"Have we met before?

"You look familiar to me," Melina said innocently as she bit into the crunchy bread.

Tawny eyes gazed at her. She could have sworn there was a smile in their depths. "I'm sure I would have remembered if we had."

Aristo leaned back in his chair, stretching out his long legs, and sipped his wine, his eyes never leaving her profile. Her cheeks were lightly sun-kissed. And her eyes... her wonderful, intelligent eyes with their thick, dark lashes. Eyes that could make love to a man or break his heart.

She turned those eyes on him now. "I love this island."

"Have you been here before?"

"Yes," she said quietly. "A long time ago. I've thought of it often."

Aristo nodded. "Yes." His voice was deep and rich. "Some places, like some people, are not easily forgotten."

Dear Reader,

Welcome to Silhouette—experience the magic of the wonderful world where two people fall in love. Meet heroines that will make you cheer for their happiness, and heroes (be they the boy next door or a handsome, mysterious stranger) that will win your heart. Silhouette Romance reflects the magic of love—sweeping you away with books that will make you laugh and cry, heartwarming, poignant stories that will move you time and time again.

In the coming months we're publishing romances by many of your all-time favorites, such as Diana Palmer, Brittany Young, Sondra Stanford and Annette Broadrick. Your response to these authors and our other Silhouette Romance authors has served as a touchstone for us, and we're pleased to bring you more books with Silhouette's distinctive medley of charm, wit and—above all—*romance*.

I hope you enjoy this book and the many stories to come. Experience the magic!

Sincerely,

Tara Hughes
Senior Editor
Silhouette Books

BRITTANY YOUNG

A Woman in Love

Silhouette Romance

Published by Silhouette Books New York

America's Publisher of Contemporary Romance

"I know my passion. It escapes me not."
—Sophocles, *Electra*

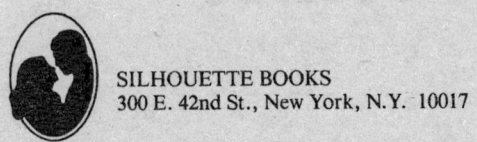

SILHOUETTE BOOKS
300 E. 42nd St., New York, N.Y. 10017

Copyright © 1989 by Brittany Young

All rights reserved. Except for use in any review, the reproduction or utilization of this work in whole or in part in any form by any electronic, mechanical or other means, now known or hereafter invented, including xerography, photocopying and recording, or in any information storage or retrieval system, is forbidden without the permission of Silhouette Books, 300 E. 42nd St., New York, N.Y. 10017

ISBN: 0-373-08658-X

First Silhouette Books printing July 1989

All the characters in this book are fictitious. Any resemblance to actual persons, living or dead, is purely coincidental.

®: Trademark used under license and registered in the United States Patent and Trademark Office and in other countries.

Printed in the U.S.A.

Books by Brittany Young

Silhouette Romance

Arranged Marriage #165
A Separate Happiness #297
No Special Consideration #308
The Karas Cup #336
An Honorable Man #357
A Deeper Meaning #375
No Ordinary Man #388
To Catch a Thief #424
Gallagher's Lady #454
All or Nothing #484
Far from Over #537
A Matter of Honor #550
Worth the Risk #574
The Kiss of a Stranger #597
A Man Called Travers #622
The White Rose #640
A Woman in Love #658

BRITTANY YOUNG

lives and writes in Racine, Wisconsin. She has traveled to most of the countries that serve as the settings for her Romances and finds the research into the language, customs, history and literature of these countries among the most demanding and rewarding aspects of her writing.

GREECE

Underlined places are fictitious.

Prologue

Melina Chase leaned her elbows on the railing that surrounded her father's research ship, *Calista*, and stared longingly at the Greek island less than a mile away.

A friendly, meaty hand ruffled her long golden hair. "What are you looking so dreamy about?"

She turned and smiled at the older man who tiredly lowered himself into a deck chair. "I didn't know I was."

"Ah, well, perhaps that's just the way fifteen-year-old girls are supposed to look."

Melina raised herself up so that she was perched on the railing facing him. "You look so tired, Dad."

"I am."

"No luck on funding?"

"Not on funding or anything else. I've never run into such obstacles as these." He looked at his daughter and shook his head. "Melina, do you realize that at this moment we're anchored above a three-thousand-year-old Greek city?"

She nodded. Not only did she realize it, Melina had helped with some of the preliminary diving work earlier in the week.

"The mind boggles at what lies buried under the centuries of sand, but the government won't budge. They don't want the site disturbed."

"Did they say why?"

"Oh, some nonsense about a curse."

Melina's eyes lit up. This was the kind of thing she loved. "A curse? What kind of curse?"

"Oh, just the usual one about bad luck befalling anyone who dares to intrude on the city's watery grave."

"Do you believe it?"

"Of course not. I don't see how any thinking man could. There's no such thing as a curse."

"The Greek government obviously believes there is, otherwise they'd let you dig here."

Gregory Chase sighed.

"What are you going to do now?"

"I guess we'll head back to Turkey."

"When?"

"Tomorrow morning."

Melina looked at her father but didn't say anything.

Gregory Chase gazed back at her, amazed at how much she resembled her mother. She was his golden girl. "What are you thinking, Melina?"

She hesitated just a moment. "I know you don't like me taking off on my own, but I'd really love to see Kortina before we leave," she said, pointing to the island behind her. "It's so lovely. Nothing will happen to me, I promise."

A corner of her father's mouth lifted. "You're growing up so quickly. I wish I didn't have to send you off to boarding school every time the academic year starts. I feel as though I miss more of your life than I share," he said wistfully. "If your mother were here, things might have been different."

Melina's mother had died unexpectedly five years earlier. "I know. But she's not, and I don't mind boarding school, really. I just wish that during the summer when I'm here on the ship, you'd let me have a little more freedom. I think you keep forgetting that I'm not a child anymore."

Her father looked at her for a long moment, then nodded. "You're right."

"I am?" Melina asked in amazement.

"You are. At fifteen you're more than old enough to go off on your own."

Melina pushed herself off the railing and threw her arms around her father's neck in a great big hug. "Thank you, Dad. You won't regret it."

He rose from his chair and affectionately pinched her chin. "See that I don't, little one, or you're going to be back in the world of chaperons."

Before he had a chance to change his mind, Melina raced off to the small launch trailing close to the rear of the ship. There was a little red motor scooter in the front that they used for traveling when they were on land. Untying the rope that held the launch to the *Calista*, she climbed in, rocking it gently to and fro as she made her way to the back of it. The single outboard engine started on the first pull. Grasping the metallic handle, Melina sat down and maneuvered the launch away from the ship with a practiced hand. She loved to go fast, and that's what she did now. The wind blew her long golden hair and the sea sprayed her sun-warmed face as the little boat bumped its way over the swells.

As soon as she got close to the beach, Melina cut the engine and easily swiveled it out of the water to keep it from getting clogged with sand. At just the right moment, she jumped out of the launch, rope in hand, and into the ankle-deep sea, sandals and all, then pulled the boat securely onto the beach. This wasn't a recreational beach. It was strictly for fishermen. Huge nets were strung out while men, women and children made repairs. Some of them looked up and smiled at this pretty blond girl, and she smiled back, calling out a friendly greeting in their own language as she pushed the scooter past them to the cobbled road that led to the nearby markets.

Melina loved the noise and color of Greek open-air markets, particularly on the smaller islands that didn't cater to tourists. Parking the scooter off to one side, she walked down the narrow street, made even narrower by the stalls with fruits, vegetables, baked goods, fish, fish and more fish and bright bouquets of flowers. Melina bought an orange and ate it as she walked and watched. The juice dribbled down her chin and she unself-consciously dashed it away with the back of her hand.

Women, for the most part, worked the stalls; older women, softly rounded, with brown skin wrinkled from years of exposure to the bright Aegean sun. Their eyes sparkled with humor and when they smiled, their strong teeth flashed whitely—though sometimes there were gaps in the white.

When Melina had finished her orange, she couldn't resist buying a fistful of wildflowers. Holding them under her nose, she made her way back to the scooter and headed up into the cool mountains she'd been admiring for the past week from the *Calista*. The road was narrow and winding, but the little scooter managed it easily. Melina's goal was to reach the top and see close up the villa that looked out over the island and sea as though keeping quiet watch. She couldn't help but wonder if it was as beautiful and serene as she'd imagined.

There was very little traffic. When she did see a car coming, Melina was careful to get out of the way.

She was heady with her first taste of real freedom. It felt wonderful. *She* felt wonderful as she rounded the curve.

The big car was coming straight at her, on her side of the road. She had nowhere to go but over the edge and down a ten-foot drop. The last thing she remembered doing was parting with her scooter and bracing herself for the impact of the hard ground as it rose to meet her.

* * *

The man who found Melina a few minutes later leaned over her. Her breathing was regular. He checked her arms and legs. Nothing appeared to be broken. But an ugly purplish bruise was forming on her temple. He pushed her silky hair away from her face to get a better look, then sat back on his haunches and watched her. She couldn't have been more than fifteen or sixteen, a good nine years younger than himself, and obviously didn't have a drop of Greek blood in her. She was so fair, and so utterly beautiful that she quite literally took his breath away.

With a gentleness that would have surprised those who knew him, the man lifted her slight form into his arms and held her so that her head rested on his shoulder. When he turned his head slightly, he could smell the perfume of the long hair that fell in a heavy sheet down her back.

Melina had a vague sensation of strong, safe arms wrapping around her and of being carried. She was taken some place cool and quiet. She could hear the sea. She could even smell it. Someone pushed her hair away from her face. A deep voice spoke softly in Greek. Melina lifted her heavy lids and found herself gazing into a pair of remarkable, tawny eyes. She'd never seen eyes that color before. And once she'd looked into them, she couldn't look away.

A smile curved the stranger's mouth and the grooves in his cheeks deepened. "Good. You're awake."

"Am I?" she asked vaguely. Everything was so strange. Melina tried to sit up, but she moved too quickly and a stabbing pain shot through her temple.

A WOMAN IN LOVE

With a gasp, she sank back against the pillows. Pillows? The last thing she remembered was falling, but now she was in a room. A bedroom. Again Melina looked at the man who sat on the bed beside her. "Where am I?"

"You're in my home," he said softly. "I found you by the side of the road."

"My scooter!" Panic echoed in her voice. "Did you find my scooter?"

"Relax." His voice was kind. Soothing. "I brought it here with you. It's rather banged up and scratched, but it still works. Do you remember what happened?"

Melina thought for a moment. "Someone in a large car came down the middle of the road. I guess whoever it was didn't see me." Her dark-lashed hazel eyes went to his. "Was it you?"

"No. I found you some time afterward."

"And you brought me here?"

"That's right."

"Thank you." Melina's eyes met his and she couldn't look away. She didn't know this man. Didn't know anything about him. And yet she was irresistibly drawn to him.

His mouth was as carved as any on a Greek statue, and a corner of it lifted now. "You're welcome. May I know your name?"

"M—" Melina thought quickly. She couldn't let her father know about this. "Mary."

"How do you do, Mary? I'm Aristo Drapano." He rose from the bed, making an effort to jar her as little as possible. "I've called a doctor. He should be here shortly. Is there a member of your family visiting Kortina with you?"

"Why?" she asked quickly, defensively.

"I'd like to get in touch with them. I'm sure they'd like to know that you're safe."

"What time is it?"

"Eight o'clock," he said without looking at his watch.

Melina heaved a silent sigh of relief. "I'm not expected back until later. No one would even be worried about me yet." That much was true. Her father wouldn't start to worry for another hour. After that, if she wasn't back in one piece and on time, she'd spend the rest of the summer with a chaperon. Just the thought was enough to make her feel suffocated.

"Are you sure?"

She had to look away. There was no way she could look into those eyes and lie. "Yes."

Those same tawny eyes narrowed slightly. He didn't believe her. "Will you be all right alone for a short time? I have some things to attend to."

"I'll be fine."

"I'll be up with the doctor as soon as he arrives."

Melina nodded and the Greek walked away.

"Thank you," she said suddenly.

He turned and looked back at her.

"You didn't have to stop to help me. I'm grateful that you did."

The Greek looked at her for a long moment, inclined his dark head and shut the door between them.

Melina lay absolutely still, not even breathing, until the sound of his footsteps was diminished by distance. Gingerly, with the caution of one who'd been burned once already, she sat up. Her head hurt, but she could live with it. Her clothes were still on, such as they were after that fall, but her sandals had been removed. She found them on the floor beside the bed and carefully slid into them one at a time.

Still on the edge of the bed, Melina looked at her surroundings. The room was enormous, furnished with beautiful, heavy Mediterranean furniture. A balcony door was open, allowing a clean breeze to blow in. She rose from the bed and stepped outside. From where she was, she could see the *Calista* anchored offshore far below. But nearer at hand something glinted red in the fading sunlight. Her scooter! Stairs led from the balcony to the ground. Melina slowly made her way down and over to the scooter. As quietly as she could, she wheeled it down the drive for twenty yards, then held her breath while she tried to start the engine. Nothing happened. She tried again. It hummed on the second try.

Melina started to leave but stopped and looked back at the villa almost regretfully, then slowly turned and rode away.

It wasn't until she was safely back on the *Calista*, the pain in her head and the ache in her mistreated body made manageable with the help of some aspirin, and with her father none the wiser—at least until he got a look at the scooter—that Melina paused to look up at the mountain. It was a dark night except for the stars dotting the velvet black sky like a handful of carelessly tossed glitter. There wasn't even a full moon.

But she could see the villa sparkling and alive with lights.

And in her mind she could still see the tawny eyes of a Greek named Aristo Drapano.

Aristo stood on the darkened loggia of his villa, his shoulder against a white pillar, a drink in his hand, and looked out at the white ship floating so gracefully on the dark sea. Why he should feel so bereft because a girl he barely knew—a child really—had disappeared without a trace, he had no idea. He only knew that he did. He was tempted to search for her, but that would serve no purpose. She was undoubtedly safely with her family by now. He was better off not knowing where she was.

He couldn't know then how thoughts of her were going to haunt him.

Chapter One

Nine years later a seaplane, its enameled metal sparkling in the bright sunlight, flew low over the mountainous Greek island of Kortina. Melina leaned forward and gazed out the window, smiling suddenly as the *Calista*, stark white against the almost painful blue of the Aegean Sea, came into view. She touched the pilot's arm and pointed. He nodded and circled the ship once before finally touching down on the water and taxiing toward it.

As Melina leaned forward to pick up her purse, her waist-length, golden hair fell forward. She swept it back with a graceful hand as she straightened. "Just pull up next to the diving platform," she called out over the noise of the engine.

The pilot taxied to within inches of the platform. A young man standing on it, decked out in full diving gear, his air tank yellow against the black of his suit, pulled open the door for Melina and held out his hand to help her alight. She looked up and into smiling brown eyes. "Craig!" Her delight was obvious. "I thought you were in Turkey."

"I was, but then your father offered me a job working on this project. It wasn't something I could turn down. What are you doing here?"

"I had a few weeks of vacation time so I thought I'd spend it on the *Calista*." She leaned over a still-wet basket and carefully removed a remarkably well-preserved ancient vase to examine it. "I'll even help if you'd like."

"At the rate we've been losing divers around here, I'd appreciate it, but you'll have to okay it with your dad."

"Losing divers?"

"I've never been on a more accident-prone dig."

"Anything serious?"

"Not yet, but it's still early," he said as he adjusted his air tank.

Melina leaned back into the plane and took out her suitcase, smiling her thanks at the pilot.

While the plane taxied away, Craig took her suitcase, climbed halfway up the ladder to the ship and heaved it onto the deck. "Come on," he said as he came back down. "I'll give you a hand up."

She let him help her up the ladder, then turned back to him. "Is my father on board?"

"Yeah. He's got a visitor right now, but I don't imagine he'll mind an interruption as long as it's you. See you later." He adjusted his mask and put the air hose in his mouth, then disappeared over the side of the diving platform.

At that moment the seaplane raced past and soared into the air. Melina raised her hand to shield her eyes from the sun and watched until it became a distant speck.

With a happy sigh, she crossed the immaculate wooden deck to the front of the ship where her father's study was. She could see him through the window, his pipe clenched between his teeth as he listened to the man who was in the room with him. Melina's gaze swerved to the other man. He was standing in front of her father's bookcase, his back to her. Her father was six feet tall, but this man was substantially taller than that. The light-colored suit he wore, with its unstructured jacket, showed off his lean muscularity. His thick hair, so dark that it just missed being black, was neatly trimmed. It seemed as though the more agitated her father got, the calmer this man became. Melina tapped lightly on the door.

Her father looked at her over the shoulder of the man and a smile lit his eyes. "Melina!" he called out as he walked to the door and opened it. "What a nice surprise. I wasn't expecting you."

She walked into his waiting arms. "I didn't know myself until yesterday. The museum where I'm working had to close down for a few weeks for structural repairs because of an earthquake, so I thought I'd come to see you."

Dr. Chase stepped away from her and cupped her face in his hands. "You look lovely."

Melina studied him more closely. He was happy to see her—and yet she got the distinct feeling he wished she weren't there. "Did I pick a bad time?"

He hesitated before he answered. "Not at all." Dr. Chase suddenly remembered that they weren't alone and turned, his arm still around his daughter. "Melina, I'd like you to meet..."

Aristo Drapano, she mentally finished for him when she got over the initial shock of seeing those tawny eyes that had come unbidden into her dreams for years. Did he remember her, as well? Melina, her heart suddenly pounding against her ribs, extended her hand and found it enveloped in a warm and solid grip.

The Greek's expression never altered as he gazed into her eyes. "Melina," he said softly.

She was mesmerized. But then her father lightly touched her shoulder and she jumped. Her hand fell to her side as her gaze dropped away from his. "I can see that the two of you are busy." Melina turned to her father and kissed his cheek. "We can talk later. I'm going to unpack now."

"I'm sorry, dear, but it looks as though I'm going to be busy well into the evening."

"That's all right. I'm going to be here for a few weeks. We'll have lots of time to catch up." Her eyes went back to the Greek. "Mr. Drapano, it was nice meeting you."

He inclined his dark head.

"Excuse me." Melina went back onto the deck. As soon as she was out of sight of the study, she leaned against a wall, put her hand over her heart and took a deep breath. Somewhere in the back of her mind she'd thought about seeing him again, but never had she expected the impact the meeting would have upon her.

The voices of men on the diving platform brought Melina out of her reverie. Straightening away from the wall, she picked up her suitcase and carried it downstairs to the same cabin she'd used since childhood. It was a comfortable room, small but not too small, just enough to be considered cozy. Her father left it the same from year to year, so in the bookcases side by side with her Nancy Drew and Victoria Holt were college texts on archaeology. Small artifacts that she'd found while a teenager and diving with her father were set on a small dresser. They weren't anything anyone else would want, but they all meant something to Melina.

She hoisted her suitcase onto the white eyelet bedspread and opened it. Melina had spent most of her life packing her belongings to travel here and there, and she was an expert. As she unpacked her things and put them into drawers and the closet, the empty spaces filled quickly. She had friends who were amazed at what she could get into one small suitcase.

When that was done, she slid the suitcase under her bed and headed down the hall to the galley. Luigi, the rotund Italian cook who'd signed on with the *Calista* crew nearly twenty years earlier, was furious about something. His belly literally quivered with rage as he paced back and forth, swearing mightily in Italian in his operatic tenor. Melina picked up a stalk of celery and sat on the counter quietly munching until he noticed her.

He did on his next turn. He stopped swearing as he stared at her, and then his arms opened wide as he headed straight for her, engulfing her in a huge hug. "My girl," he said affectionately as he stood back and looked at her. "What you doing here? Your daddy don't tell me."

Melina smiled affectionately. "He didn't know. What are you so upset about?"

Luigi had to think for only a moment, and then his round face got red. He picked up a sheet of paper and waved it furiously in the air. "This isa why I'ma mad."

Melina took it from him and read what appeared to be a shopping list. "Groceries?" she asked, not comprehending.

"Two weeks ago I hire on thisa man to be my..." He searched for the word.

"Assistant?" Melina suggested helpfully.

"Yes, my assistant. Today I tella him I need these things froma the market for dinner tonight. He understand. He say fine. He take care of it. Well, he left two hours ago, but he don't take the list. He don't take the list, I don't havea the food, the crew don't have its dinner."

With new eyes, Melina looked over the list again. "Would it help if I went to Kortina and got these things for you?"

"Oh, honey, you justa got here. I can't ask you to do something like that."

"You didn't ask. I offered. Besides, I'd like to go to Kortina and look around. It's been years since I was there."

"But what about your father?"

"He said he was going to be busy for quite a while."

"You sure, Melina?"

"I'ma sure, Luigi," she said, affectionately imitating his Italian accent the way she had when she was a child.

Luigi gently pinched her cheek and wiggled it back and forth. "I say it before and I say it again. You're a good kid. If I were thirty years younger..."

"Yes?"

"I'da still be too old."

Melina laughed as she slid from the counter, the list in one hand and what remained of the celery in the other. "If my father asks where I am, tell him I went into Kortina."

"I'll do that." Then he went back to muttering to himself in Italian. "And then I'ma gonna fire my so-called assistant," he yelled as he shook his finger in the air.

She definitely didn't envy the reception that poor assistant was going to get when he finally showed up. Luigi's wrath was a thing to behold—and avoid.

Melina popped the last bite of celery into her mouth as she climbed the staircase to the upper deck. Without looking when she got to the top, she turned the corner and crashed headlong into Aristo Drapano. He caught her shoulders in a firm, steadying grip. "I'm so sorry," she gasped in surprise as she looked up at him.

Aristo's hands dropped to his sides. "It's all right. Where are you going in such a hurry?"

"Kortina." Melina folded the grocery list and put it in the deep front pocket of her white sundress. Aristo wasn't touching her any longer, but she still felt as though he were. "I have some errands to run for our cook."

"I was just leaving myself. I'll take you."

"That's not necessary, really. Besides, I have to be able to get back here."

"I'll make sure that you do. Come." He walked to the side of the ship and climbed down a ladder to his boat, then held his arms up for Melina.

She hesitated only a moment before hiking up her full skirt and backing down the ladder. Aristo's strong hands encircled her slender waist and lifted her the last few feet to the speedboat. While she sat in a comfortable swivel seat at the front of the boat, Aristo turned the key that started the powerful engines. Melina watched him as he removed his jacket and tossed it over the back of his chair, but remained standing himself. His suit pants were loose-fitting with pleats, belted at his flat stomach. He loosened his plain tie and unbuttoned his big light blue shirt at the throat and cuffs, then rolled his sleeves up, exposing his tanned forearms. Her gaze moved to his long-fingered and strong hand as he put the boat into gear and steered clear of the ship. Within moments he'd shifted twice and they were thumping across the waves toward Kortina.

Melina, with the warm wind blowing in her face and her long hair billowing out behind her, raised her eyes to his profile. It was classically Greek with straight lines that seemed almost carved. He looked to be in his mid-thirties, which would have made him about twenty-five the last time they'd met.

Aristo turned his head suddenly, as though sensing Melina's scrutiny. She met his look with a direct one of her own. They remained like that for several seconds. Then Aristo looked away to steer the boat.

They went straight to a dock that had been built since the last time Melina had been there. As the boat approached, Aristo called out to two boys sitting with their feet dangling over the edge. He tossed a rope to each of them, and they tied them securely. Then Aristo took his suitcoat from the chair, jumped out and held Melina's hand to steady her while she climbed out.

"Where do you need to go first?" Aristo asked.

"To get some vegetables at the market."

One of the young men followed about ten paces behind, stopping when they stopped, walking when they walked. Melina turned to look at him and then looked at Aristo. "What's he doing?"

"I've asked him to deliver your purchases to the *Calista* for you."

"I can do that myself."

"Not if you're having dinner with me."

Melina's eyes flew to his. "Am I?"

"That's up to you."

Her hesitation was fleeting at best. Melina wanted very much to spend some time with him. "Then I guess I am."

It was late in the afternoon and business in the marketplace was winding down. Melina took the list from her pocket and made her purchases item by item. The *Calista* had a running account with the vendors, so no money changed hands. The boy following them would wait until his arms were filled, then run to the boat, drop them off and come back for more. When they were all finished, Aristo gave the young man very precise instructions, then put his hand under Melina's elbow as they walked to a taverna with white-clothed outdoor tables and a view of the sea and the anchored *Calista*.

"Do you like Greek wine?" he asked as he held out a chair for her.

"Yes." She looked at him over her shoulder. "In fact, I haven't had any retsina for a long time."

As soon as Aristo took his seat across from her, a waiter arrived. Aristo ordered a bottle of retsina, then turned his attention to Melina. "I heard you tell your father something about the museum you were working on. What is it that you do?"

"Lots of different things, such as classifying and dating artifacts found on digs and attempting to piece together the broken ones."

"I assumed that you were more interested in the finding of the artifacts, like your father is."

"Oh, I am. I particularly enjoy the underwater work. But I do that more for fun these days."

The waiter arrived with the bottle of wine, poured them each a glass, then left.

"What do you do for a living?" Melina asked as she sipped the cool, almost clear liquid that tasted slightly of pine.

"I have various business interests, mostly in Athens, none of which have anything to do with archaeology." He looked out at the *Calista*. "She's a beautiful ship."

Melina followed his gaze and nodded. "My father bought her when I was a baby. It took him years to outfit her just the way he wanted for his work, but it was worth it."

"Did you spend much time on board?

"I grew up there," she said softly. "My father took my mother and me everywhere with him until she died."

"And then what happened?"

"I had to go to boarding school for most of the year, but I still spent my summers on the ship."

The waiter returned with a basket of thickly sliced grilled bread and a dill and cucumber spread. Aristo fixed a slice and handed it to Melina, then fixed another for himself. Melina watched him, wondering not for the first time if he remembered her at all. She decided to probe a little. "You look familiar to me," she said innocently as she bit into the crunchy bread. "Have we met before?"

Tawny eyes gazed at her. She could have sworn there was a smile in their depths. "I'm sure I would have remembered if we had."

Melina took another bite of bread. His answer was really no answer at all. She dropped the subject. "How did you come to know my father?"

"We just met today. The people of Kortina are concerned about what he's doing and they asked me to speak with him."

Melina remembered the conversation she'd had with her father years ago. "Does their concern have something to do with the curse that's supposed to follow anyone who tampers with the ruins?"

"Precisely."

She looked at him curiously. He seemed such a rational man. "Do you believe in it?"

At that moment the young man who'd helped them with the groceries approached their table. He told Aristo in Greek that he'd delivered everything safely and that Aristo's boat was docked where it had been earlier.

"Thank you," Aristo said as he handed him a large bill from his wallet.

The youngster beamed and ran off.

"It was nice of you to do that for me," Melina told him.

He looked at her for a moment and then went back to their earlier topic of conversation. "I believe you asked me if I thought there was really a curse."

Melina nodded.

"What I believe doesn't matter. The fact is that there have been several accidents already, and your father's only been on the site for a month."

"But I was speaking to a diver just today and he said that none of the accidents have been serious."

"Not yet," Aristo said ominously.

"Do you think that's going to change?"

His gaze was unwavering. "I'm not a fortune teller, Melina, but I'd say that the likelihood of something serious happening is great. Unfortunately, by the time your father moves on, it might be too late."

"My father is a very sensible man, contrary to what you apparently think." Melina wasn't angry, but she felt a point needed to be made. "The safety of the people who work for him has always been his primary concern. As far as unearthing the landmass that broke away from Kortina all those thousands of years ago, he obviously doesn't believe there's any threat."

Aristo studied her quietly. "If it helps any, I like your father very much. He's a good man."

Melina suddenly smiled and Aristo's heart caught at the beauty of it. He inclined his head toward the small menu the waiter had left when he'd seated them. "What would you like to eat?"

"Moussaka," she said without looking. "I haven't had that for longer than I can remember."

Aristo discreetly signaled the waiter and ordered the same thing for each of them while Melina watched the sun slowly set behind the sea. He leaned back in his chair, stretching out his long legs, and sipped his wine, his eyes never leaving her profile. Melina was what he'd call a very natural American beauty. She seemed to have been born for the outdoors. Her hair was bright and golden, with heavy silken strands that begged a man's hand to touch it. Her nose was straight and just right for her face, with a smattering of freckles. Her cheeks were lightly sun-kissed. Her mouth was beautifully defined with a hint of rosy color, curving up at the corners, and her eyes... Her wonderful, intelligent green-blue eyes with their thick, dark lashes were eyes that could make love to a man or break his heart.

She turned those eyes on him now. "I love this island."

"Have you been here before?"

"Yes," she said quietly. "A long time ago. I've thought of it often."

Aristo nodded. "Yes." His voice was deep and rich. "Some places, like some people, are not easily forgotten."

Melina's mouth parted softly as her breathing grew more rapid. God, he was an attractive man.

"Aristo! There you are," said a man in Greek. "I've combed the island looking for you."

Aristo held Melina's gaze for a moment longer, then the spell was broken. "Hello, Timon," he said to the newcomer, his voice neither friendly nor unfriendly. "What's so urgent that it couldn't wait until later?"

The man, a younger, paler version of Aristo, turned a chair backward and sat down, resting his forearms along the back of it. "Helen called," he explained, his appreciative gaze on Melina. "She wants you to pick her up in Athens tonight rather than tomorrow. Who are you?" he asked Melina without pausing.

Aristo sighed. "Melina Chase, this is my brother Timon Drapano."

Melina extended her hand, and Timon raised it to his lips. "You're American?"

"Yes."

"What brings you to Kortina?"

"I'm visiting my father on the *Calista*," she said, retrieving her hand.

"Chase," he repeated. "Of course. Did you speak with her father?" he asked his brother in Greek.

"Yes, he did," Melina answered in the same language.

Timon had the grace to look embarrassed. "Sorry. Where did you learn to speak our language so well?"

"I spent a lot of time in Greece as a child."

"I'll have to watch what I say around you."

The outdoor taverna was filling up with Kortinians. The talking and laughter grew louder, and casually dressed local musicians played Greek music while the people clapped to the beat.

Timon looked at his brother. "I told Helen that you'd come to get her. She's waiting."

Aristo looked at Melina, and Timon followed his gaze. "Don't worry. I'll see that she gets back to the *Calista* safely."

Aristo still hesitated. "Is that all right with you, Melina?"

She would have preferred Aristo, but she nodded.

He sensed her feelings. "I can call her to say that I'll be late."

"No, please don't." She smiled reassuringly. "I'll be fine with your brother."

His eyes rested on hers. "We'll see each other again." It was a statement. Not a question.

Timon looked from one to the other. "Of course you will. At the party we're having tomorrow night."

Aristo said nothing.

Timon smiled at her. "In fact, I'll escort you."

"I really hadn't planned—" Melina began, only to be cut off by Timon.

"I know you're here to visit with your father, but surely you can have one night off to enjoy yourself with people your own age. I'll pick you up at eight. You don't even have to consider it a date. I'll simply be your means of getting there and getting home."

Timon was charming and Melina gave in. "All right."

Aristo's expression gave nothing away as he rose. "Then I'll see you tomorrow, Melina. Good night."

She watched him leave. "Who's Helen?" she asked before she could withdraw the words.

"His fiancée," Timon said matter-of-factly. "They're getting married in about a month."

Melina felt as though she'd been stabbed.

The waiter arrived with two Greek salads and two moussakas. Timon smiled at her. "Not only am I the recipient of my brother's good taste in women, but I get his dinner, as well."

Suddenly she wasn't very hungry.

"Eat, Melina," Timon said gently. "The food here is the best in all of Greece."

She did manage a little, and it was wonderful. Timon turned out to be good company and a very nice man. It was almost ten o'clock when he dropped her off at the *Calista*. She climbed up from the diving platform and stood on the deck, watching while the speedboat headed home through the dark sea, its running lights dancing over the waves. The island flickered with lights in the background.

"Did you have a nice evening, Melina?"

She turned and saw that her father was reclining in a deck chair, smoking his pipe. Melina walked over to him and kissed his cheek, then stretched out in a chair next to him. "Yes."

"Aristo Drapano is an interesting man."

She nodded in the darkness.

"A mysterious man."

Melina turned to look at her father. "In what way?"

"Knowing him becomes a matter of deciding whether he's a thief—or whether he isn't."

"What a curious thing to say. I don't understand."

"About four months ago one of the banks he owns was robbed of about ten million dollars in gold bricks."

"Ten million dollars?"

Her father nodded. "It didn't belong to him, of course, but to some foreign company whose name escapes me at the moment. Apparently the gold was being transferred from one of Drapano's banks to another and was stolen en route. Since Aristo himself was the only one who knew the complete details of when, where and how the gold was being transported, he's believed by the authorities to have had a hand in its disappearance."

"That's ridiculous!"

Her father looked at her in surprise. "Melina, you hardly know the man well enough to decide what he's capable of doing or not doing."

"Perhaps not technically, but my intuition tells me that he would never do anything like that."

Gregory Chase nodded. "To be honest with you," he said quietly, "so does mine, otherwise I would have come to Kortina to get you the minute I discovered that you'd left with him. I just thought you should be aware of what's going on."

Silence fell between them.

Gregory Chase suddenly reached over and squeezed Melina's hand. "I wish I could stay up longer with you, but I'm a tired old man who has to start his day very early in the morning."

Melina smiled. "I'll help you tomorrow."

"You don't have to. This is your vacation. You should relax and enjoy yourself."

"Diving is relaxing to me."

"As you wish." He rose, then leaned over and kissed the top of her head. "Don't stay up too late."

"I won't."

She watched her father as he walked away. "Dad? I love you."

He turned and looked at her through the darkness. "I love you, too, Melina. Good night."

She leaned back in her chair with a sigh. The light breeze coming off the sea was cool, but Melina welcomed it. She could see the lights of the Drapano villa in the distance and wondered if Aristo was back from Athens yet. With his future wife.

His future wife.

She had met the man once before. Just once. Why should she care whether he was getting married or not?

But she did. Very much.

Chapter Two

Melina awoke early the next morning and slipped into her bathing suit, then put on over it her pink shorty wet suit. Her long legs were bare, but that's the way she preferred it when she was diving in warm water. As she was brushing her hair back into a ponytail, there was a knock on the door. She opened it and found Luigi standing there holding a tray with orange juice and toast on it. "Your papa tell me that you're gonna dive today."

She smiled at him as she finished putting the band around her hair. "And you wanted to make sure I had something to eat before I went."

"That's right. I knew you wouldn't if I didn't bring it to you myself."

She kissed him on the cheek as she took the tray from him. "Thank you, Luigi."

"It'sa not much, but you make sure you eat it."

"I will."

"Every bite."

"I promise."

Leaving her door open, Melina set the tray on her dresser, picked up the juice in one hand and the toast in the other and headed for the upper deck.

It was a glorious day. She walked to the railing and stood for a moment with her eyes closed, face raised to the sun.

"Melina, over here," her father called.

With a smile, she crossed the deck to her father's worktable where he was busy with four other divers. The only one she recognized was Craig.

"Melina, this," her father said as he pointed to a grid on the papers spread before him, "is where you'll be working."

She studied the layout until she got her bearings in relation to the ship and nodded. "How deep is it?"

"It varies. Anywhere from sixty to a hundred and twenty feet. Pericles," he indicated a young Greek man standing next to Craig, "will be working close to you, but not with you. He's a volunteer from the island and his main job is to clear debris."

Pericles smiled at her and she smiled back, then examined the chart again.

"Craig will be here," Dr. Chase continued, pointing at the far end of the chart, "Doug here and Cyril here."

The way it looked, Pericles was going to be the only one near her.

"I'll be coming down myself periodically to see what's going on. To begin with, Melina, I just want you to use the portable suction lift. It's already there. Concentrate on your particular grid, clearing it layer by layer. I know there's a floor of some kind where I have you working, but I don't know what kind or if it's even something we're interested in. We won't know that until we get some of it uncovered. Most of what we've found so far has been in pieces, which isn't surprising considering that the land met its end because of an earthquake and tidal wave, if we can believe Plato's very secondhand version of events. Any questions?"

No one said anything.

"All right, then, head out. Melina, I had your air tanks filled and your equipment brought up from storage. They're on this deck near the diving platform."

"Thank you."

As the others took off, Gregory Chase handed her a waterproof chart on a weighted clipboard and an attached pen. "You won't be coming across much at first, but as you well know, everything has to be documented."

Melina nodded.

"This is a lot like old times, isn't it?" her father asked as he gazed at her.

"Yes. I keep thinking back all those years to when we were first here. How did you manage to get the Greek government to agree to this? They used to be so opposed."

"Believe me, it hasn't been easy. It's taken almost ten years of negotiation to come up with an agreement we could all live with. The truth is, they still aren't thrilled, but I think when they see what we recover for them, that will change."

Melina finished her juice and set it on a table. "Speaking of recovering things, I guess I'd better get started."

"You be careful."

She smiled reassuringly at him as she went to the other end of the ship. Her equipment was right where her father had said it would be, right down to the fins. Her white tanks glinted in the sun. She put only one on, leaving the other on deck in a shady corner, picked up her chart and pen and made her way down to the diving platform. Craig was just going off the edge. After wetting down her mask and adjusting her air regulator, Melina did the same, walking straight off the platform and into the sea. The water closed around her with a rush and flurry of bubbles as she sank. For a few moments, as her descent stabilized, she treaded water and looked around to get her bearings. She had no problem seeing. The water was clean and clear and the bright sun shone straight down. She spotted Craig swimming away from her and then she spotted Pericles, already at work on the floor of the sea.

Using her fins, she propelled herself downward until she reached the spot her father had pointed out on the grid. Pericles looked over at her and nodded his head, acknowledging her presence, then went back to work.

The suction lift was like a large vacuum cleaner, but so light underwater that it was easy to maneuver. Melina picked it up and began clearing off her grid, layer by monotonous layer. Every time she came across what looked like something of value, she numbered the item and penned the number on her chart in its precise location.

Nearly an hour had gone by when Pericles caught her attention. He made an upwardly spiraling motion with his finger to indicate that he was going up. Melina looked at her pressure gauge, saw that she still had more time and held up her hand to indicate that she'd be up in about five minutes. He seemed strangely uneasy about leaving her alone, so she gestured more firmly that she'd be up shortly and he should go on without her. Even though she was twenty-five, her father, in his own way, was still having her chaperoned. The thought made her smile.

In exactly five minutes, she propelled herself up to the diving platform. Craig was there and gave her a hand up. She raised her mask to sit on top of her head and removed some of her equipment, handing her empty tank up to Pericles. He then handed her the full tank.

For the rest of the day, into the early evening hours, this became the routine. After nearly eight hours, Melina had come across only a few shards of pottery. Certainly no floor. As she surfaced for the final time that day, she found herself on a crowded diving platform. Unhooking her tank, she handed it up to Pericles, then took off her fins and held them in her hand while she climbed the ladder to the upper deck. Craig came up immediately after her, and smiled. "You look tired."

"I am."

"You've gotten soft from all that easy museum work you've been doing."

Without answering, Melina opened the zipper of her wet suit and collapsed onto a deck chair. Craig sat next to her, and the two of them let the sun warm them.

"That water gets cold after a while," Craig said.

"Uh-huh," Melina agreed without opening her eyes.

A peaceful silence fell between them.

"I'm glad it's the weekend," Craig said after a few minutes had passed.

"Are you doing something special?"

"Just going into Athens with the rest of the crew. But I'm not setting a foot back on the *Calista* until late Sunday night. What about you?"

"I'm going to a party tonight on Kortina, but then I'm coming back here. Early," she added. "I feel as though I could sleep for a week."

"Melina," her father said from above her.

She opened her eyes and shaded them from the sun with her hand.

"I'm sorry to do this to you, but I have to go to Athens tonight. I won't be back until Monday."

"Is anything wrong?"

"No. Just some things I need to take care of. What time are you going out?"

"Eight."

"Then we can still have dinner together." He patted her shoulder and walked away.

Both Craig's and Melina's eyes followed him. "Do you know what's wrong?" Melina asked when her father was out of earshot.

"He's worried about funding. This curse garbage follows him everywhere he goes. It makes private institutions reluctant to give us any financial help."

"You'd think that as a society we'd have moved beyond that kind of thing by now."

Craig nodded. "But people have long memories. They still remember what happened to the men who invaded King Tutankhamen's tomb in Egypt. People laughed about the supposed curse, but then one by one the research team died—or were killed. Sometimes under truly bizarre circumstances."

"I remember reading about that."

"And now the Kortinians are reporting that they see strange lights coming from beneath the water."

Melina shook her head. "Strange lights. I wonder what started that rumor?"

"Who knows? Someone probably saw reflected moonlight or something and distorted it beyond all recognition. I've been out here for more than a month and I've never seen anything."

Melina sat up with a sigh. "Well, I'm going to go shower the seawater out of my hair and put on some real clothes."

Craig smiled at her. "Have fun at your party tonight."

"Thanks. And you have a nice weekend."

"I intend to. See you Monday."

When Melina got to her cabin, she stripped out of her wet suit and bathing suit and climbed into a hot shower. The spray stung her face and shoulders, but it felt good. Invigorating. She soaped her long hair and leisurely rinsed it, then soaped the rest of her body and let the spray of water wash over her until the foam made its way down the length of her body.

Almost reluctantly, she stepped out onto a bathmat and dried herself with a big towel, which she then wrapped around her torso, tucking the end between her breasts. She blew her hair dry and left it falling in a straight sheet to her waist, then went to her closet to see what there was to wear. She had brought two good dresses with her. The one she chose now was a black taffeta with a bustier top that left her shoulders bare and flared out at the waist to the middle of her knee. The only jewelry she wore was a pair of black onyx earrings circled by two rows of diamonds that had belonged to her mother. Before leaving her room, the last thing she did was step into a pair of black high heels that made her already long legs seem even longer. When she got to her father's study, he rose from behind his desk and whistled appreciatively. "I'm so used to seeing you in your working clothes that I'd forgotten what you look like when you're dressed up." He walked to a small table set near a window and held a chair out for her. "Luigi brought our dinner a moment ago."

Melina sat down and removed the cover from her plate, smiling when she saw that he'd fixed her favorite—broiled salmon. "He never forgets anything."

"Not when it comes to you. He thinks of himself as your second father."

Still smiling, she took a bite and sighed. "I'd almost forgotten how good his cooking is."

"I won't tell him you said that."

Melina laughed. But then she grew quiet. All day she'd had trouble getting Aristo Drapano out of her mind, and now that she was about to see him again she found it even harder to think about anything else. Without realizing it, she began moving her food around her plate, no longer interested in eating.

Her father suddenly reached out and covered her hand with his to stop the motion. "What's wrong, Melina?"

She looked up, startled at first, and then smiled. "I guess I'm a little preoccupied."

"With what?"

"Lots of things. Nothing important."

"Are you sure?"

"I'm sure."

Her father frowned for a moment and listened. Melina heard the plane at the same time. "I think that's mine," he finally said when it was obvious that it had circled the ship. "The others have already gone." His eyes rested on his daughter. "One of these days before you leave here, the two of us are going to have to make the time to actually have a long conversation." He shook his head as he put the cover back on his half-eaten dinner. "Try to eat a little more of your salmon or Luigi will have a stroke."

Melina obediently took another bite.

Her father picked up his suit coat and slipped it on, then snapped the lid of his briefcase closed. "I'll be back Monday afternoon at the latest."

"All right."

"You take good care of yourself."

"I will."

He winked at her and smiled, then disappeared through the door.

Melina took a few more bites of her salmon and gave up. Putting the cover over her plate, she walked out onto the deck and looked around. She could see a boat approaching in the distance and knew it was Timon. As he pulled alongside the ship, she climbed down the ladder.

"A woman who's on time," he said as he helped her down. "I like that."

Melina sat in the same seat she had when Aristo had been piloting the boat. "What a sexist thing to say."

Timon grinned. "We Greek men aren't known for our liberated attitudes."

"I've heard rumors to that effect."

"Believe them." He slammed the boat into gear and headed toward Kortina—not the more populated part, but around the island where the villa was. The sun had just begun to set, so the sky was still quite light, but filled with a profusion of colors that grew richer and deeper as the minutes passed.

Timon pulled the boat up at the wooden dock and jumped out to secure it with ropes before holding out his hand to help Melina alight. She stood on the dock, looking out over the sand, then up at the sheer cliff. "May I ask an idle question?"

"Of course."

"How do you propose getting us up there from down here?"

"That's a good question."

"I thought so when I asked it."

"Don't worry, I'm not going to make you climb."

"That's something of a relief. What exactly *are* you going to make me do?"

"Come on." He took her hand and they headed across the beach.

"Wait." She stopped, and leaning one hand on his shoulder for support, took off her high heels. "Now I can walk."

They went on until they came to a large basket. Timon climbed in and then held out his arms for Melina.

She stood where she was, the heels of her feet firmly planted in the sand as she looked at him. "What's this?"

"A basket."

"I can see that it's a basket. Why are you in it?"

"Because it's going to take us to the top of the cliff."

"You mean it's going to take *you* to the top of the cliff. I'm going to stay here where it's safe and watch."

"Coward."

"I'm just smart."

"I designed it myself. It's perfectly safe, believe me. We've been using it for years."

Melina shook her head and sighed. "The things I'll do to get to a party." Moving closer, she dropped her shoes into the basket and let Timon lift her up and over the edge. "What now?"

"We go up." He took a remote control that looked like a garage door opener, aimed it upward and pressed a button. The heavy cables attached to the basket creaked as they tightened, and the basket slowly began to move. "It's just like an elevator," he explained.

"What do you do if you get stuck halfway up?"

"I don't know," Timon admitted with a frown. "We haven't had that problem yet."

"Wonderful."

It was slow going, which was fine with Melina. After three minutes or so, the basket ascended into a hole that had been cut through the part of the cliff that jutted out like a pouty lower lip and stopped inside a small shed that had been built around it. Timon hopped out easily. Melina scooped up her shoes and let him lift her to the safety of the ground.

"There," he said with a smile. "That wasn't so bad, was it?"

"It was—interesting." She leaned on him again while she slipped on her shoes. "And there's no way in the world I'm getting on that thing again."

"Honestly, Melina, the more you ride in it, the easier it becomes. Even my grandmother's gotten used to it."

"Is she going to be here tonight?"

"Yes. She's visiting for a month or so."

"Then she and I are going to have a talk."

"Don't you believe me?"

"Should I?"

He grinned at her. "All right. She's not quite used to it yet, but she's getting there." He took her hand in his and led her out of the shed and along the lighted garden paths to the villa. People flowed through the huge doors and onto the lawn, talking and laughing. White-jacketed waiters made their way through the people taking drink orders while women wandered among the crowd with trays of food. Chamber music drifted from one of the inner salons and wound its way around the yard.

Without her realizing it, Melina's eyes searched for Aristo even while Timon held her hand.

And she found him. He was standing off to the side, looking elegant in his dark tuxedo, a drink in his hand, talking to a tall woman with short dark hair and big gold earrings. She was very Greek and very lovely.

Timon followed her gaze. "That's Helen."

She'd known it without his telling her. They made a striking couple.

Aristo spotted Melina at almost the same time. Their eyes met and held across the lawn. He stopped what he was saying in midsentence, causing his fiancée to look first at him and then at Melina to see what he found so interesting. Then she lightly touched his arm and he turned back to her.

Melina watched for a moment longer, then turned to Timon. "Does Aristo give lots of parties?"

"Not really. He's not a very social person."

"I wouldn't have guessed that."

"It's true. Of course, Helen's just the opposite. She lives for society and wants Aristo to escort her. That's why he spends so much more time at his place in Athens than he does here."

A man joined Aristo and Helen. Aristo whispered something to Helen, then left her with the other man and crossed to Melina. He gazed down at her, his tawny eyes missing nothing. Though he didn't say the words, his look made her feel beautiful.

His eyes moved to her hair. "I'm glad you left it down."

"After what I went through to get here, if it hadn't started out that way, it would surely be down by now," she said dryly.

He smiled.

Timon had been speaking with someone else, but he now turned to Melina. "What would you like to drink?"

"Mineral water."

"Mineral water?" he repeated in surprise. "I can see that you're really going to cut loose tonight." With a shake of his head, Timon walked away from them.

"While he's flagging down a waiter," Aristo said as he warmly took her arm in his hand, "I want you to meet our grandmother." He led her across the lawn to where a lovely woman who appeared to be in her late seventies was sitting watching the people around her. "Grandmother," Aristo said, "I'd like you to meet Dr. Chase's daughter, Melina." He placed Melina's hand into that of his grandmother. "Melina, this is Anthea Drapano."

Melina, her hand still in the gentle clasp of the older woman's, sat on a chair facing her. She liked her immediately.

"Melina," the woman repeated softly. "That's a very Greek name for such a pale girl."

"My parents were having a love affair with Greece when I was born."

"I commend their taste. And from what I hear, your father still is."

"Yes."

"He's making a lot of people very uncomfortable."

"Are you one of those people?"

Anthea Drapano gently lifted her shoulders. "Let's just say that I lack your father's curiosity about those who've gone before us."

Melina smiled. "You would have made a terrible archaeologist."

The woman smiled back at her.

"There you are," Timon said as he walked up to her carrying their drinks. "Hello, Grandmother. You're looking splendid this evening." He leaned over and kissed her cheek. "Excuse me while I spirit Melina away. There are some people I want her to meet."

Melina would have liked to have stayed with her longer, but Timon was tugging on her, and rather than be rude, she excused herself and went with him.

Aristo leaned his broad shoulder against a pillar near his grandmother's chair and watched.

"She's lovely," his grandmother said.

"Yes, she is."

"Timon seems quite taken with her."

"He'd be a fool not to be."

"And you disapprove?"

There was a short silence. "I'd hate to see her get involved with him."

"Afraid he'll break her heart?"

Aristo paused before he answered. "Something like that."

"Unless I read her wrong, I don't think he'll get the chance to do that."

He was silent.

"Is there something more that concerns you?"

"Nothing that I can't handle."

"And nothing that you intend to discuss with me, apparently."

With a smile curving his mouth, he leaned over and kissed his grandmother on the forehead. "Not yet."

"Does it have something to do with Melina?"

"Only in that her presence complicates things somewhat," he said as he straightened away from her.

Anthea studied Aristo's profile. "Is it that she complicates things—or that she herself is a complication?"

His eyes rested on Melina's slender back. "Word games."

"Perhaps. Which is it?"

"A little of both, I suppose." He looked down at her. "You're far too observant."

"I'm getting old, Aristo. Watching people is something I've become very good at lately. I see things these days that in my youth I would have missed."

"Such as?"

"Such as the way you looked at Melina when she first arrived with Timon—and the way you're looking at her now."

"She's an attractive woman. I appreciate attractive women. Don't read anything into that."

"I don't have to. It's all there for me to see."

"Grandmother," he said affectionately, "I confess that I've sometimes been surprised by the accuracy of your insights, but this time you're wrong."

"Am I really?" She didn't sound convinced.

"I'm getting married in four weeks."

"To a woman with whom you're not in love."

"I have a great fondness for Helen."

"Fondness isn't love."

"Sometimes it's better. More steady. Less confrontational. Helen's going to make a fine wife, a fine mother."

"As long as you hire someone else to take care of the children."

"You did."

"I was a fool." She shook her head. "Oh, Aristo, your future unfolds before me like an empty canvas."

"I thought you liked Helen."

"What I feel for her isn't important. It's what you feel that matters."

"She's Greek."

"True enough."

"I've made promises to her. I've given my word to her family."

"Also true. But that was before Melina came."

"Grandmother, you have a one-track mind."

"I just want you to be happy."

"I will be. I've waited a long time to get married. Helen is exactly the kind of wife I want. I don't need someone like Melina Chase..."

"*Complicating* things?" she suggested.

"Exactly."

Anthea Drapano smiled to herself. He might not need it, but that's exactly what had happened.

Aristo narrowed his eyes into the darkened distance where he saw a man quietly signaling to him. "Excuse me," he said suddenly, walking away without further explanation.

Melina politely let Timon introduce her here and there, but she wasn't feeling nearly as happy as he was and his insistent laughter and chatter began to grate on her nerves. Her gaze wandered over the other guests. A movement in the trees caught her attention, and she strained to see what was there. Two men. One of them was Aristo. The other was a very large man, as tall as Aristo, and perhaps a hundred pounds heavier. Whatever they were talking about must have been important, because the two of them were very intent on their conversation.

"Melina," Timon said, "will you excuse me for a short time? I see someone I need to speak with."

"Of course."

"Just make yourself at home."

It was almost with relief that Melina watched him approach a young Italian woman she'd met earlier. The two of them put their heads together. He said something and she giggled.

Free at last, Melina ducked through the other guests, unaware of the tawny eyes watching her, and made her way through the gardens to the cliff where she stood looking out at the sea. She could see the *Calista* anchored in the distance, its lights reflecting in the water.

Aristo stopped a few yards behind her and just watched as the wind lifted her silky hair, rippling it over her bare shoulders and down her back. Other than that, she was absolutely still.

Moving away from the cypress trees, he came up behind her. Melina knew who it was without turning. His warm hands closed over her cold bare arms, and she was suddenly filled with something she could only describe as an ache.

"You should have something on," he said softly. "It's a chilly night."

She turned her head slightly and looked up at him. "I'm fine, really."

Aristo removed his jacket and draped it over her shoulders. "There. Now you're fine."

Melina turned and looked up at him as she pulled the ends of the jacket together over her breasts. "Thank you."

"Don't you like the party?"

"It's lovely."

"If it's so lovely, why are you off here all alone?"

"I just needed to get away from the noise for a few minutes."

Aristo gazed at her without speaking.

Melina found his scrutiny disconcerting. "Shouldn't you be with your other guests?"

"My other guests are fine. It's you who seem somehow discontented."

"Discontented?" Melina shook her head. "I apologize if I gave that impression. I think perhaps I'm just tired."

"Any particular reason?"

"A very particular one. I was diving all day and I'm not used to it."

Aristo stiffened. It was something Melina sensed more than saw. "I thought you were here on vacation."

"I am. But I like to dive and I haven't done much of it lately. I'm afraid my expertise tends to confine me to stuffy museums."

"I'm surprised your father let you with all of the accidents that have occurred."

"He knows I'm a careful diver. He trained me himself." A yawn sneaked up on Melina before she could disguise it. "I'm sorry," she said with an apologetic smile.

A corner of his mouth lifted. "That's all right. Would you like to go home now?"

Melina nodded. "Yes, but I have to find Timon first."

Aristo had seen him disappearing into the gardens with the other woman. "Unless I miss my guess, you won't be seeing Timon until much later. I'll take you home."

"But what about Helen?"

"She won't miss me for the few minutes I'll be gone. Come on."

The two of them headed for the nearby shed. As Aristo put his hands at Melina's waist to lift her into the basket, he felt her stiffen. "What's wrong?"

"I really don't like this thing."

He lifted her in anyway, then climbed in beside her. "I'll keep you safe."

It was strange, but Melina believed him and she relaxed. "The next time I go anywhere, I'm bringing my own transportation. That way I can take myself home."

"Without having to depend on anyone else."

"Exactly."

Her back was close to his chest, and when he spoke his breath moved her hair. "Don't you like to depend on other people, Melina?"

A delicious shiver went through her. "I don't mind—if it happens to be someone I trust. But frankly, it's easier being independent. Particularly at times like this."

When the basket touched down, Aristo lifted Melina out first, then joined her on the sand.

"Just a minute," she said as she started to take off her shoes the way she had earlier with Timon.

Aristo suddenly scooped her up in his arms and carried her across the beach to his boat, gently setting her inside.

Melina tried desperately not to feel what she was feeling, and it was in silence that they crossed the bay to where the *Calista* was anchored.

Aristo pulled up beside the ship. "I hope the crew isn't too noisy so you can get some rest."

She rose and moved to the ladder. "That won't be a problem tonight. I'm all alone."

Aristo's eyes narrowed. "Alone?"

"Everyone's in Athens for the weekend."

"Are you saying that your father left the ship unattended?"

"Except by me."

"He's a very trusting man, isn't he?"

"Anything that's important has been locked safely away."

"Still, there should be someone besides you on the ship. I'll send one of my men over to stay with you."

Melina looked at him curiously at first, but then a lovely smile curved her mouth. "Aristo, you worry too much about someone you hardly know."

His eyes roamed over her shadowed face as the small boat gently rocked. The look made her heart beat faster. "That's my prerogative."

"Well, it's nice of you but unnecessary. I'm perfectly capable of taking care of myself. Besides, I enjoy being alone. Nothing is going to happen."

Aristo offered no further argument as he gave her a hand up the ladder and watched until she reached the safety of the deck.

"Oh, wait," she called down as she removed the jacket from her shoulders. "I forgot to give you this."

Aristo took it from her outstretched hand, his eyes on hers. "Good night, Melina."

"Good night."

She watched as he restarted the engines and pulled away from the ship, then wearily went to her cabin and to bed. As tired as she was, though, Melina had trouble sleeping. She kept thinking about Aristo Drapano.

When Aristo got back to the villa, he moved quickly through the gardens and found Helen near the house. She smiled when she saw him. "Aristo, there you are! I have to go back to Athens. I think I told you that I start a new modeling job early tomorrow morning."

"You did. Would you mind if I sent you back with a pilot instead of my taking you?"

Helen moved closer. "Are you sure that's what you want to do?" she asked softly. "You could always spend the night in Athens."

Aristo gazed into her dark eyes. "Not tonight."

Her arms circled his neck and her mouth drew closer to his. "Come on," she coaxed.

It was strange, the things he suddenly noticed. She wore a lot of makeup, and in all the time he'd known her, he didn't remember ever seeing her without it. Her hair was perfect. Not a strand out of place. And her perfume... he'd never really thought about it before, but it was a little heavy.

Her lips touched his. Aristo returned the kiss, but his heart wasn't in it.

Helen sensed the difference immediately and stepped back. "What is it? What's wrong?"

He shook his head. "Nothing important. I guess I just have other things on my mind."

Another man approached them in the darkness. "Nicholas." Aristo sounded almost relieved. "I'd like you to take Helen to Athens."

Helen looked curiously at Aristo for a long moment. "You'll call me?"

"Yes."

"Promise."

"Of course."

She kissed his cheek. "Try not to miss me too much."

He watched her walk away and wondered at his complete lack of reaction. He wasn't in love with Helen any more than she was in love with him. But he'd never failed to find her attractive before now.

With a shake of his head, Aristo went into the villa and changed out of his tuxedo and into comfortable pants and a cable knit sweater. As he hurried out of the villa and along the garden paths, avoiding the guests, Timon's voice suddenly came out of nowhere.

"I understand you took Melina home for me while I was otherwise occupied."

Aristo stopped and turned. Timon was standing in a clearing, his shoulder against a tree, a cigarette in his hand. "That's right."

"I guess I should thank you."

"That's not necessary."

"No. I suppose it isn't." Timon's voice was thick with drink. "I don't imagine you found it at all bothersome."

Aristo said nothing.

"Melina's very lovely."

Still Aristo said nothing.

Timon looked his brother over, his relaxed pose belying the tenseness beneath the surface. "The party isn't over yet. Where are you off to in such a hurry?"

"I'm going out in the boat."

"At this hour?"

"I feel like fishing, Timon. Do you have a problem with that?"

"Fishing? It's a little late, isn't it?"

"It's amazing what you can catch in the dead of night." Aristo's voice was almost menacingly quiet. And with that he walked away.

Timon threw his half-smoked cigarette to the ground and rubbed it hard with the toe of his shoe, then turned on his heel and returned to the party.

A WOMAN IN LOVE

Aristo anchored his boat about forty feet away from the *Calista*. Leaning back in the comfortable chair, he stretched his long legs out and got ready for what he hoped would be a quiet night.

Melina tossed and turned until she simply gave up trying to sleep. Throwing back her sheet, she left her room and climbed the stairway to the upper deck. With a tired sigh, she leaned her forearms against the railing and stared at the twinkling lights of the island.

A boat gently bobbed in the bay. Looking closer, she realized that it was Aristo's boat. What was he doing there?

Chapter Three

Aristo stayed until the last vestiges of sunrise had disappeared, then turned his boat toward home. As he approached the villa on foot, he saw Timon sitting on the loggia, still awake, a cold drink in his hand.

"Catch anything?" Timon asked.

Aristo stopped in front of him. "Not yet. But there's always tonight, and the next night, and the next."

"What exactly is it that you think you're going to find out there?"

Aristo just looked at him, his expression carved in stone. Without saying anything, he turned and walked into the villa.

Timon's fingers tightened dangerously on the glass he was holding.

A WOMAN IN LOVE

* * *

Melina had fallen asleep on a deck chair. The sun was already warming her skin when she finally awoke. She raised her arms high over her head and stretched luxuriously. Then, suddenly remembering why she was on deck in the first place, Melina rose abruptly and walked to the railing. Aristo's boat was gone. But she hadn't dreamed it. His boat had been there the night before. The question was why? To protect her? Why did he feel so strongly that she'd need protection? Protection from what? From whom?

With a delicate shrug of her shoulders, Melina went to the lower deck and put on a pair of jeans and a short-sleeved white blouse, got herself a glass of orange juice from the galley and went back to the upper deck to enjoy the sunshine.

Leaning her elbows on the railing, she watched the other boats. Some were recreational—even the hardworking fishermen liked to play on the water on weekends—and she waved at a water-skier who zipped past about a hundred feet away.

Up on the cliff, glinting in the morning sunlight, sat the Villa Drapano. No matter how hard Melina tried not to look at it, her gaze, and her thoughts were repeatedly drawn to those pale stones. Was Aristo there now?

Turning away, she went to her father's library and sat in front of his worktable to go over his sketches of what lay beneath the ship. Using an advanced type of sonar that echoed back images, he'd shadowed in areas where he thought remnants of the lost part of Kortina were to be found.

This had become a passion of her father's over the years. Even as a child she had seen his eyes light up at the very mention of this place. The lost Kortina was his Atlantis.

Melina had so little time here before going back to her own work on Cyprus, and she wanted very much to help her father. Going down to the property room where the diving equipment was kept, Melina checked her tanks to make sure they'd been filled. They were ready to go so she put on her wet suit and gear and walked off the diving platform into the sea.

Recreational divers rarely went alone, but divers who worked underwater didn't have the luxury of that restriction. Too often there was no one else, or if there was, he worked in a different area. Melina had worked alone many times before and felt no qualms about it now as she used her fins to propel herself to her grid. The suction lift was waiting for her and she lifted it easily in her arms to begin the work of cleaning off another layer of sand.

She became so absorbed in her work that she didn't see the boat overhead as it docked next to the *Calista*.

She worked quite contentedly for about thirty minutes when she noticed that breathing was becoming more difficult. Looking at her watch, Melina saw that she should have at least another half hour of air, so she jiggled her regulator and took another breath. It was even more difficult. Then she looked at her pressure gauge. It registered half full. She took another breath and suddenly realized with horror that there wasn't any more air and she had to swim at least ninety feet straight up before she could get some. Forcing down the panic that instinctively welled in her throat, Melina automatically unfastened her weight belt and let it fall to the floor of the sea as she rhythmically moved her feet. She knew better than to go too fast because the last thing she wanted to do was get the bends, but she didn't have the luxury of taking her time. There was simply no air left and it became a choice between the bends and suffocation. She began moving her feet as fast as she could in a desperate effort to propel herself to the surface before she passed out, ripping off her mask along the way.

When she finally broke the surface, her chest felt ready to explode and she was choking on swallowed water. It was all she could do to keep herself afloat. Somewhere in the distance she heard someone call her name, and then strong arms were around her, pulling her toward the diving platform and dragging her onto it. Melina lay on her side, coughing and gasping for air. A gentle hand stroked her wet hair away from her face.

When she was able, Melina, still breathing as though she'd been running in a marathon, turned her head and found Aristo looking down at her. Water dripped onto her from his drenched clothes and his breathing was every bit as ragged as hers.

"What the hell happened?" he panted as he helped her to sit up and remove her tank.

"I don't know. I should have had plenty of air, but I ran out without any warning."

"Didn't you check your gauge?"

If looks could kill. "I've been diving since I was a child. Of course I did. Look at it for yourself."

Aristo picked it up and gazed at it for a long moment while a dark frown clouded his brow. "It's broken. When was the last time you used it?"

"Yesterday." She took off the rest of her equipment, but as if the effort were too much, she lay back on the platform, still breathing hard, and put her hand over her aching chest. "I didn't think I was going to make it."

Aristo leaned over her and looked into her eyes. "Are you sure you're all right, Melina?" he asked gently. "Do I need to get you to a doctor?"

Melina shaded her eyes from the sun and gazed back at him. "I'm fine. Or at least I will be in a few minutes. Thank heavens you were here."

Aristo's jaw clenched. "Who has access to the air tanks?"

"Who has...?" she asked blankly. "Why, everyone on the crew."

"Anyone else?"

Melina shook her head. "No. We fill them on board."

He picked up her gear and put it onto the ship, then helped Melina to her feet and up the ladder. "Go and change. I'm taking you with me."

"Taking me where?"

"To my home."

"I'd rather stay here."

"And I'd rather you were someplace safe."

She turned to him as soon as she was on the upper deck but waited to speak until he'd climbed up to join her. "Aristo," she said quietly, "this was an accident. The odds of something like this happening again are infinitesimal. Besides which, I'm not going back into the water today."

"That's right, you're not. You're going home with me."

Melina wasn't used to being spoken to in such a domineering tone and she didn't like it. "You don't tell me what to do."

His tawny eyes were unblinking as they looked into hers. "You're very headstrong."

"Headstrong? Is it headstrong not to like someone I barely know ordering me around as though I'm his property to command?"

"Is that how I sound to you?"

"Yes."

"Then I apologize."

His words took Melina by surprise. Aristo Drapano didn't strike her as the kind of man who apologized either easily or often. "Thank you."

"The reason I'm here in the first place is because my grandmother enjoyed meeting you last evening and wanted you to visit with her this morning. She thought you might even like to stay for lunch."

"That's very nice of her."

He waited for a moment as he watched her. "Well? What's your answer?"

Melina looked around the ship. "There are a few things I wanted to do around here."

"I'll wait."

"All right," she sighed. "I'll shower and change. It won't take long."

As soon as she'd disappeared below deck, Aristo picked up the pressure gauge and looked at it more closely. There was no obvious tampering, but even disconnected from the tank it read half full.

When Melina came back up, she'd changed into loose pink shorts and a pink blouse, belted at her waist. Her hair was damp. "I'd offer you some of my father's clothes," she said as she realized he was still wet from his plunge into the sea, "but nothing of his would fit you."

"I'm fine." He took her hand and helped her down the ladder and into his boat. Aristo immediately went back on the *Calista* and then returned, carrying the tank and gauge in his hand.

"Why are you bringing those?"

Aristo set them down in the back of the boat, then moved to the front next to Melina and started the engines. "I have to go into Athens today. I'll take them to a shop there and have them repaired."

Melina looked at him in surprise. "I'm sure you have better things to do with your time than that. Please don't bother."

His eyes met hers. "It's no bother."

Expecting no argument and receiving none, Aristo put the boat into gear and headed across the sea. Once again they went to the Drapano dock, and once again Melina had to get into the damn basket.

She looked at him as the basket ascended the cliff. "Have you ever heard of something called steps?"

"We have steps. But they're very steep and there are a lot of them."

"Well, next time you take the basket and I'll take the steps and meet you at the top."

Aristo smiled at her. "Stop complaining."

"It's what I do best when I don't know what's going on—through no fault of my own."

The basket reached the top and Aristo lifted her out, then climbed out himself. Together, they walked through the cool gardens. Aristo looked at Melina and saw that she was smiling. "What is it?"

"Oh, I was just remembering how, years ago when my father had docked the *Calista* about where it is now, I used to look up here and wonder what it was like. There was something so peaceful about the villa."

"And now that you've seen it close up?"

"I think it has the potential to be the way I imagined it, but there's some kind of undercurrent at the moment."

"Undercurrent?"

"Yes. It's calm on the surface, but there's a storm going on below."

"Ah. Anything else?"

Melina hesitated only a moment. "Look, I should tell you that I know about your problems."

"My problems?"

"The gold being stolen."

"I see. Word gets around quickly."

"My father told me the day I arrived."

Aristo was silent.

"He thought I should be aware of it."

Aristo stopped walking and turned to face her. "And yet you came to the party last night and you're here with me today. Why is that?"

"I trust you."

The muscle in his jaw clenched. "Brave words, considering that you barely know me. I could be the biggest crook on the island for all you know."

Melina shook her head. "You'd never do anything like that," she said softly.

Aristo reached out and caught her chin between his thumb and forefinger. "Don't be so naively trusting, Melina. It could get you in trouble."

Her blue-green eyes met his. "I'm neither naive nor too trusting, Aristo. But I feel as though I know you. As though I know your soul. I realize that sounds silly. I can hardly believe I said it. But it's what I feel."

"It doesn't sound silly at all." He moved his hand to cup her cheek. His thumb moved over her smooth skin as he gazed down at her. "Oh, Melina," he said quietly, "what am I going to do about you?"

She looked at him without saying anything.

Aristo's head slowly lowered toward hers, his eyes on hers all the way. When their lips finally touched, Melina felt the contact all through her body. He was achingly gentle as his mouth explored hers, never pulling her any nearer to himself than she already was. Their bodies didn't touch. He lifted his mouth from Melina's and gazed into her eyes before lowering it to hers again, searching, tasting. His hand moved around to the back of her head, his fingers tangling in her thick hair as the kiss grew deeper and deeper.

"No," he suddenly moaned as he pulled away from her. "I can't do this."

As soon as he did that, Melina remembered Helen. "I'm sorry," she whispered, stricken.

The expression on her face tore at Aristo's heart. He wrapped his arms around Melina and held her for a moment in a comforting embrace. "You have nothing to be sorry about," he said softly against her fragrant hair. "I'm completely to blame. It won't happen again."

She reluctantly backed away from him.

Aristo, trying not to look at her, picked up the air tank from the ground. "Let's go."

Timon was leaving the villa just as they approached. He looked at Melina in surprise, then his eyes drifted to the air tank his brother was carrying and back to Melina. "What are you doing here?"

"Your grandmother invited me."

"How strange. I just spoke with her and she didn't say anything about your coming here."

"Perhaps," Aristo said, "she didn't feel she needed to clear the visit with you."

Melina's gaze moved from one to the other. They were so alike—and yet so different. And there was very definite tension between them. Much more so than on her first night when they were both at the taverna.

"And did she also want to see Melina's scuba equipment?" Timon asked as he inclined his head toward the tank.

"It's broken. I'm taking it to Athens to be fixed."

He lifted a skeptical brow. "I see. Well, I hope you have a pleasant day."

"Where are you going?" Aristo asked.

"Out."

"Out where?"

"Since when am I accountable to you?"

The muscle in Aristo's cheek tightened.

"Goodbye, Melina," Timon said as he walked around them and headed for a car parked not far away.

"What was that all about?" Melina asked quietly as they crossed the loggia.

Aristo shook his head, and that was his only answer.

Without asking any more questions, Melina followed him into the villa. They found his grandmother in the dining room, reading a newspaper and having some breakfast. She smiled in pleased surprise when she saw Melina. "Good morning, dear."

Melina returned the smile.

"Please, have a seat." She turned her attention to her still damp grandson. "What happened to you?"

"I just got a little wet." Aristo held out a chair for Melina. "Grandmother, I have to go to Athens this morning. I'll probably be back sometime late this afternoon."

She looked at him curiously, but said nothing as he left the room.

A half-embarrassed smile touched Melina's mouth. "You weren't expecting me, were you?"

"As a matter of fact, I wasn't, but I'm no less happy to see you because of that."

Melina turned to look at the now empty doorway through which Aristo had disappeared. "I wonder what he's up to?"

"Up to?"

"Why would he tell me that you wanted to spend the day with me when you obviously had no intention of doing any such thing?"

"I stopped trying to attribute motives to men years ago. Would you like some coffee or tea?"

"No, thank you."

Anthea picked up her cup and saucer and rose. "Let's sit on the loggia. It's such a lovely morning."

Melina followed her through the white French-paned doors to the loggia just beyond. The view from here was completely different from that at the other end of the villa, with mountains looming in the distance.

The two women sat in blue-cushioned wicker chairs, a small table between them. "It's lovely here, isn't it?" asked Anthea as she looked at Melina.

Melina nodded and she gazed into the distance.

"I confess I miss it when I'm away," Anthea said softly.

"Away?"

"I spend a few months a year here. The rest of the time I live in Athens."

"You prefer the city?"

"It's not a matter of preference. It's the place of my birth. Most of my friends live there—at least those who are left. Growing old can be a lonely business."

"You have your family."

She smiled. "Yes. My grandsons bring me great joy. But that's not what I'm talking about. I miss old friends who are no longer here. We were young together and shared common experiences. Do you understand?"

"Yes, I think I do."

Anthea reached over and touched Melina's hand. "I knew you would. You have an old soul."

"It's strange that you should say that." Melina's voice was softly reminiscent. "My mother used to tell me the same thing when I was a child."

"Perhaps it's because of growing up around your father's work. Or perhaps you really do have an old soul."

"I wonder." She gazed at the mountains. "Sometimes ancient Greece is so real to me that it's hard to believe I wasn't actually there."

"Maybe you were."

Melina smiled as she shook her head. "I think I just have a very vivid imagination."

A helicopter flew directly overhead and immediately disappeared from view as it passed over the villa.

"There goes Aristo."

"Does he go to Athens often?"

"A few times a week. That's where he keeps his business offices. He has an apartment there as well. And, of course, that's where Helen lives." She looked at Melina from the corner of her eye as she said the last part.

"There you two are," Timon said as he walked out of the villa.

Anthea turned her head and smiled. "Hello, dear. Did you pick up your boat?"

"I did. It's docked and ready for action." He turned to Melina. "What about it?"

"What about what?"

"Do you water-ski?"

"I used to."

"Then you still do. It's like riding a bicycle." He leaned over his grandmother and gave her a kiss on the cheek. "You don't mind if I steal Melina away from you for the afternoon, do you?"

Anthea tried to look stern, but failed miserably. "I most certainly do. We're having a lovely chat."

"Then you come with us."

"With you? On a boat? The way you drive? Never."

Melina looked at him suspiciously. "If your own grandmother won't get on a boat with you, what makes you think that I will?"

"Optimism."

Anthea shook her head. "You might as well go, dear. Timon will keep at you until you agree to it."

"But I didn't bring a bathing suit."

"We have some here for guests, but if you don't like that idea, I can always take you to the *Calista*."

Melina looked at Anthea and laughed. "You're right. He doesn't take 'no' for an answer."

"You didn't say 'no,'" Timon reminded her with a grin. "You said that you didn't have your bathing suit."

"It looks like I'm going skiing." Melina rose. "But I'd like to get my own skis."

His eyes widened in mock surprise. "Your own skis? I think we have a ringer here. Come on. I'll take you to the *Calista*."

They walked around the house and through the garden to the shed. This time though, Melina didn't get into the basket. "Where are the steps?"

"The steps?" he asked blankly.

"Aristo told me there are some steps that lead down to the beach."

"Oh, but, Melina, it's such a long way down."

"That's how I feel every time I climb into that basket. Now, where are the steps?"

He walked her to a ledge about fifteen feet from where they were standing. The steps were tiered, about ten steps to each tier, and she couldn't see how many tiers. They were overgrown with bushes and weeds, but Melina was undeterred as she started down them. Timon wanted to charm her, but not badly enough to take the stairs. He climbed into the basket and lowered himself to the beach.

Melina arrived a few minutes after he did, slightly out of breath but smiling. Looping his arm through hers, he walked her past Aristo's boat to a bright red speedboat tied next to it. "Is this yours?" she asked as she climbed inside.

"Uh-huh."

"Is it new?"

"No. I've had it for about a year, but it's been in the shop for the past week."

Timon sat in front of the controls and started the powerful engines with a burst of noise as Melina sat next to him. "Hang on," he yelled as he moved the boat away from the dock. A moment later the boat thundered across the bay at what would have been the land equivalent of eighty miles per hour.

Melina liked speed, but this made her nervous. Her hands gripped the sides of the burgundy leather seat so tightly that her knuckles turned white.

There was no time for conversation, even if they'd been inclined to make it. It seemed as though they'd no sooner left the dock than they'd arrived at the *Calista*. Melina reluctantly loosened the grip of her numbed fingers.

Timon laughed as he watched her. "Did I make you nervous?" He sounded almost hopeful.

"Don't be silly. I've always enjoyed watching my life flash before my eyes." Melina swiveled around in the chair and crossed the boat to the ladder leading up to the deck of the *Calista*.

"Would you mind if I leave now and come back for you in a few minutes?" Timon asked.

"Not at all. It'll probably take me that long to find my things."

She started to leave, but turned back. "You aren't going to try to break any speed records while I'm skiing, are you?"

He looked shocked. "Melina, you wound me."

"I just asked a question. And I still want an answer, wounded or not."

"All right. I'll go slow and easy."

She looked skeptical.

Timon crossed his heart. "Trust me."

Melina just smiled. He was a perfectly nice man, but she wasn't at all sure she trusted him. In the next moment, though, she remembered that he was Aristo's brother and she transferred some of the trust she felt for Aristo to Timon. "All right. I'll be ready by the time you get back."

"Great. It's a perfect day for being on the water."

Melina looked out at the crystal blue skies and the smooth water. He was right. It was lovely.

Without saying anything else, she climbed up the ladder to the *Calista* and stood near the railing to watch as Timon and his boat shot across the bay to the village. He was like a little boy inside a man's body. A lot of women would find that appealing, but Melina, strangely, did not.

Going down to her cabin, Melina put on her bathing suit and her shorts over it, then went to a storage room in the bowels of the ship and dug around until she found the skis her father had had made for her when she was sixteen. Shouldering the skis and a bag with a towel and a fresh change of clothing, Melina went back to the upper deck and looked over the side. Timon hadn't returned yet, so she leaned the skis against the railing and put her bag down. Just as she was about to sit in one of the deck chairs, she heard a noise on the ship. It wasn't particularly loud. Just a noise that shouldn't have been there. Melina turned in the direction from which she thought it had come and listened intently. A moment later she heard it again.

Moving as quietly as she could, she crossed the deck and headed toward her father's study. Suddenly everything around her seemed particularly hushed. Even the sea.

Melina stopped every few steps and became as still as a statue, suspending even her breathing, and listened. Then she moved a little further and stopped again.

Despite the heat of the day, Melina felt goose bumps rise on her flesh. Something wasn't right.

She edged toward the study, and when she was there, moved close to the wall. Her heart was pounding as she leaned over to look through the glass.

A large hand suddenly reached out of nowhere and clamped down on her shoulder. A scream tore from her throat.

Chapter Four

"What are you doing here?" asked the man in Greek as he turned her around roughly.

Melina found herself staring up at an enormous man with an unpleasant face. The same man Aristo had been speaking with at last night's party. To her surprise, she was more angry than afraid as she shook off his hand. "What am *I* doing here?" she asked, also in Greek. "I think the more pertinent question is what are *you* doing here?"

"I'm the new assistant cook, Lambus."

"The new assistant...? Oh!" Melina put her hand over her pounding heart. "I wasn't expecting anyone else to be here." She extended her hand. "How do you do, Lambus. I'm Melina Chase, Dr. Chase's daughter."

He took her hand in a firm grip and immediately released it. There was no smile.

"I heard a noise and didn't know what it was," she explained. "That's why I was sneaking across the deck. Are you going to be staying on the ship?"

"Yes, ma'am."

"Is there anyone else here with you?"

"Luigi."

"Is he here now?"

"In his cabin."

"I see." She gave him a half smile as she walked around him. "I think I'll just have a quick word with him before I leave."

Going below again, she went to Luigi's cabin and knocked on the door. He opened it almost instantly and beamed at her. "Melina! I wasa wondering where you were."

"I've been on Kortina. Luigi, I wanted to ask you about the new cook you hired."

"Ah, yes. Lambus."

She nodded. "I just met him on the upper deck. Was he recommended by Aristo Drapano?"

Luigi looked confused. "No."

"How did you find him, then?"

"Of all things, he founda me. And I'll tell you something. He knows his business."

"Did you check his references?"

"Just one on Kortina."

"And it wasn't Mr. Drapano?"

"No. It was from the owner of some little taverna in the village."

"I see." She wondered why, if Lambus knew someone as influential as Aristo Drapano, he hadn't used him as a reference.

"Is something the matter, Melina?"

She smiled reassuringly. "No. He just surprised me on deck a little earlier and I wanted to make sure he belonged here."

"He's a hard worker," Luigi told her. "Maybe not the friendliest guy ina the world, but he's not here to win a Mr. Congeniality contest."

"True."

"Are you going to be on the ship today?"

"No. I'm going water-skiing. But you're going to be here, right?"

He nodded.

"Good. I know you trust Lambus, but I'd prefer that he not be left on board alone."

"You worry too much," Luigi told her affectionately as he pinched her cheek. "You just go have fun."

When she got back to the upper deck, Lambus was nowhere in sight, but Timon was back. He'd already put her skis into his boat and grinned up at her as she climbed down the ladder to join him. "Ready?" he asked.

"As ready as I'll ever be."

There were a few other boaters out, but not many as they made their way further into the bay where the water was smooth.

"You go first," Timon called out over the noise of the engines.

Melina slipped out of her shorts and blouse and dived over the side as soon as the boat stopped. Timon handed her her skis, then dropped the tow rope into the water for her. As soon as Melina was ready, she gave a shout and Timon took off, slowly at first, picking up speed until she was on her feet and skimming neatly across the water. She was amazed at the ease with which she regained her feel for skiing after an absence of years. Soon she was crisscrossing back and forth in the wake left by the boat.

Timon glanced over his shoulder every few seconds to make sure she was still up.

Her first run was a long one, and her knees grew tired from the exertion. Melina signaled him to stop, and Timon gradually slowed the boat down, allowing her to sink gracefully back into the water. Circling around, he picked her up, then went over the side for his turn.

He was good, and quite a show-off as he skied backward on one foot, the other foot hooked in the tow rope. He took a few spills but always came up laughing.

They skied until late afternoon. As Timon helped her back into the boat for the last time, she collapsed onto a seat and tilted her head back. "I'm exhausted!"

"I'm hungry," Timon added.

Melina nodded.

"Let's go to the villa and have some dinner."

Melina turned her head and looked at him. "Thanks, but no. I've imposed on your grandmother enough for one day."

"It's not an imposition. She loves the company. Besides which, I'm leaving you no choice." Putting the boat into gear, he headed across the bay to the Drapano dock.

Melina stood on the beach and looked from the basket to the stairs.

"What's wrong?" Timon asked as he tied up the boat.

"I'm a woman in conflict."

"About what?"

"I don't want to go in the basket, but I'm too tired for the stairs."

"Then there's no conflict. You'll have to go in the basket."

With a reluctant sigh, Melina crossed the beach and climbed in. Timon aimed his remote control and up they went. As soon as they arrived safely, Melina climbed out, a smile touching her mouth.

"What's so amusing?"

"I have this strange urge to drop to my knees and kiss the ground every time I make it out of that basket alive."

"I swear to you, Melina, it's as safe as walking. Safer."

She lifted a brow expressively, but said nothing as they started down the garden path.

As soon as they reached the villa, Timon bounded up the staircase waving for Melina to follow him. She did, to a comfortable guest room. "You can shower and change in here," he told her. "I'll meet you downstairs in about half an hour."

The bathroom had everything anyone could want, and Melina took a leisurely shower, then blew-dry her long hair and dressed in the white pants and summer sweater she'd packed in her shoulder bag. If she'd known she was going to be having dinner here, she would have picked something a little more appropriate than simply dry clothes to go on over a wet bathing suit. But, she thought as she looked into the mirror with a shrug, there was nothing she could do about it now.

When she got downstairs, there was no sign of anyone. Melina stood on the loggia and looked around, then started down the garden path.

"Melina!"

She turned, startled, and saw Anthea Drapano cutting fresh flowers and putting them into a basket on the ground next to her. "Be a dear and help me with this, will you?"

Melina walked over to her and lifted the basket. "They're beautiful."

The older woman nodded, the clippers still in her hand, as they began walking. "I love flowers." She glanced sideways at Melina. "How was your day with Timon?"

"Fun."

Anthea stopped to cut a long stemmed, bright yellow flower and added it to the basket over Melina's arm. "Timon is nothing if not fun." Her voice was full of affection. "Now, Aristo, on the other hand, takes life much more seriously."

"I can tell."

"Not that there's anything wrong with that, mind you. I just wish he'd allow himself more time to relax and enjoy himself."

Melina smiled. "My father said that to me just yesterday and I found myself explaining to him that I enjoyed working and found it relaxing."

"Perhaps the same is true with Aristo." She lifted her shoulders in a delicate shrug. "All the same, I know that he's missing out on things most men his age have had for years."

"Such as?"

"Such as a family of his own."

"Well, he'll be married soon." Melina tried to sound casual, but the fact was that she'd never found anything so difficult to say in her entire life.

"Yes."

They stopped again. This time Anthea snipped a white flower and held it to her nose for a moment before adding it to the basket.

Melina became lost in her thoughts.

"Melina?"

She jumped and looked at the woman next to her. "Excuse me?"

"I didn't mean to startle you, dear."

"I'm sorry. I have a bad habit of daydreaming at awkward times."

The older woman smiled. It was the smile of someone who knew a pleasant secret. "Let's go back to the villa. You're staying for dinner, I hope."

"Timon invited me."

"Good. If he hadn't, I would have."

Timon still hadn't come downstairs when they got back to the villa. Anthea pointed to a round table holding an empty vase in the center of the foyer. "Set the basket there, Melina, please." Then she looked at her hands. "I'm going to wash up. Would you mind arranging the flowers for me?"

"I'd enjoy it."

"You should find fresh water already in the vase."

Melina checked. It was full. Using the clippers, and humming as she worked, she snipped some of the longer stems as she artfully settled the flowers one by one into the vase.

She was unaware of the man watching her until she stepped back to admire her handiwork.

"It's lovely."

Turning, she found Aristo standing behind her, his arms folded across his powerful chest, his shoulder leaning casually against the doorframe. Her heart made its now familiar movement within her chest. "Thank you."

Pushing away from the doorframe, he reached behind him and picked up a stainless steel air tank. "I brought this back for you."

Melina moved closer. "It's not mine."

"I got you a new one."

"But why?"

"It seemed a safer thing to do than repairing the old one."

"What was wrong with it?" she asked as she took the new tank from him.

"The nozzle on the tank was apparently bumped and bent, and the pressure gauge was damaged."

"That's odd. Everything was just fine yesterday."

"Are you sure no one but the crew had access to those tanks?"

"Yes."

"What about when you were off the ship?"

"Everything was locked in the property room. No one from the outside could have gotten in. Besides, why would anyone want to tamper with an air tank?"

Aristo looked at Melina for a long moment, then took the tank from her and leaned it against the wall. "I don't know that anyone would. Like you, though, I find it curious that the same equipment that worked fine yesterday nearly got you killed today."

"Nearly got you killed?" Timon asked as he crossed the foyer to stand next to Melina. "What are you talking about?"

Aristo's level gaze met that of his brother. "When Melina was diving this morning she ran out of air. There was no warning and her gauge registered an incorrect reading."

A silent tug of war seemed to be going on between the brothers. Aristo was completely calm while Timon grew more agitated. "Is that why you took her diving gear to Athens?"

"I had Spiro check things out."

"And what did he find?"

"He couldn't be sure it was tampered with, but he also couldn't eliminate the possibility." Aristo's eyes never moved from his brother's face. "What do you think happened, Timon?"

"What do I...? How would I know?" He turned to Melina. "You didn't say anything when we went skiing this afternoon. Are you sure you're all right?"

"I'm fine, really. It was just lucky that Aristo was there because I don't think I could have made it back to the *Calista* on my own."

Timon dragged his fingers through his hair, obviously upset. "Excuse me." Without saying anything else, he abruptly left the foyer and walked down the hallway. A moment later a door slammed in the distance.

Melina looked at Aristo, bewilderment in her eyes. "What was that all about?"

"Nothing that concerns you."

"I beg to differ. If what's going on between the two of you has something to do with what happened to me this morning, I'd say that it concerns me very much."

Aristo reached out and gently cupped her face in the palm of his hand. "This isn't something I can talk to you or anyone else about at the moment. Just believe me when I say that I won't let anything happen to you."

She put her hands over his. "Aristo, you're frightening me."

His eyes held hers. "That's not my intention."

"I'm leaving," Timon said as he came back into the foyer. "I don't know how long I'll be gone."

Without waiting for anyone to respond, he walked out the door. Melina stared after him. "Is it me?"

"Is what you?" Aristo asked.

"You brought me over here this morning and promptly left and now Timon invites me to dinner and *he* leaves."

Aristo smiled. "This time I'll stay."

She looked at him suspiciously.

"I promise. What can I get you to drink?"

"Iced tea."

"All right. You go sit on the loggia and I'll be right back."

Melina did as she was told, sinking comfortably onto the cushion of a wicker couch. From here, she could see the Aegean. From every side of the villa there seemed to be a different and magnificent view.

Aristo returned a moment later with her tea, and something with liquor in it for himself. He sat in a chair across from her, his eyes on her profile. "What are you thinking?"

"About how beautiful your home is. I like the way the loggia runs completely around it. On this side is the sea; on the other side are the mountains. Over there are the gardens. Something for every mood."

"And what mood are you in at the moment?"

"Contemplative."

"About?"

"Nothing terribly profound. I was just thinking that all my life I've traveled. My only home has been the *Calista* and wherever she happens to be at the moment. Because of that, I've always thought that staying in any one place for very long would bore me. But I'm not bored here. I've loved this island from the moment I laid eyes on it, and if one were to try to imagine the perfect home on the perfect island, this would be it."

"All it's missing is children," said Anthea Drapano as she stepped onto the loggia and sat next to Melina. "Where's Timon?"

"He had to leave."

She shook her head. "That boy. You're going to have to speak with him, Aristo."

"He doesn't listen to me. What can I get you to drink, Grandmother?"

She looked at Melina's glass. "Tea would be lovely."

Aristo inclined his head toward the two of them and disappeared into the villa.

The fact that Melina's eyes followed him wasn't missed by the older woman. "So, Melina, where will you be going when you leave the *Calista* after your vacation?"

Melina sipped her tea.

"Back to Cyprus to work in the museum there."

"What exactly are you doing?"

"Classification, mostly, and reconstruction. For years they've been collecting pottery and statuary, most of it broken, but they haven't been able to afford to hire a professional to piece it all together and classify it until recently."

"And you're the one they chose."

"I'm the one who applied for the job."

"Don't be so modest."

"I'm just being honest."

"Well, your work sounds fascinating. I'm curious though. Why are you doing that rather than helping your father with his work?"

"I accepted the job in Cyprus before permission came through for my father to work here. I couldn't leave the museum in the lurch."

"I suppose not."

Aristo returned with the tea, handed the glass to his grandmother and sat across from them.

"Does that mean that when your work is finished in Cyprus you'll be joining the crew on the *Calista*?" Aristo asked.

"I haven't thought that far ahead."

The sun finally lowered itself into the sea, leaving them in pleasant darkness except for the light shining onto the loggia through the windows of the villa. The day noises had changed to the soft sounds of the night. A man stepped outside. "Dinner is ready," he said in Greek.

"We'll have it out here," Aristo told him.

"Yes, sir."

Within minutes a cloth had been placed over a nearby glass-topped table, a candle lit and table settings laid.

The three went to the table. Aristo seated his grandmother first and then Melina. His hands lightly—and no doubt accidentally—brushed against her shoulders as he moved her chair closer to the table.

Melina looked up at him over her shoulder. Their eyes met and held. She didn't have to ask herself why his slightest touch had such a devastating effect on her. She knew why. And if she were honest with herself, she'd known since she was fifteen. Maybe, subconsciously, that was why she felt the way she did about Kortina. Because this was where Aristo Drapano lived.

Lowering her eyes, she turned her attention back to the table as she opened her napkin and placed it on her lap, deliberately not looking at Aristo again as he sat across from her.

The same man who'd announced dinner returned now with their salads and chilled white wine.

Melina and Anthea spoke quietly as they ate, but Aristo was quietly thoughtful, at times almost unaware that others were present. A full moon was on the rise. It hung low in the sky, so large and clear that one could see shadows where craters were carved into the surface. As it moved higher in the sky, its silvery light gently fingered its way across the water, beckoning the onlooker with its beauty.

One course was removed, another served. Anthea kept looking at her grandson, concern etched in her expression. Melina watched him as well, wondering what was causing his preoccupation.

After a dessert of baklava and some strong, sweet coffee, Anthea put her napkin on the table and rose. As Aristo began to rise as well, she put her hand on his shoulder. "Please, stay seated. I'm going to read for a while and go to bed. I'll see you in the morning."

Turning to Melina, she leaned over and lightly kissed her on either cheek before straightening and smiling at her. "I hope I'll see you tomorrow as well. Good night, dears."

Melina watched her disappear inside the villa. "I like your grandmother."

His eyes rested on her with surprising intensity. "She likes you as well."

Melina turned to look at him. "What do we do now?"

"Excuse me?"

"Well, I was rather foisted upon you tonight by Timon and you've obviously got something on your mind more important than making small talk. I'd offer to take myself home, but once again I'm without transportation."

Aristo picked up his wine and leaned comfortably back in his chair, his eyes never leaving hers. "And if I want you to stay?"

Her mouth still burned from his kiss that morning. "Do you?"

"Whether I do or not doesn't matter," he said softly. "You shouldn't."

Melina lowered her gaze. "I know."

"What did you and Timon do today?"

That was an abrupt change of topic. "I think he mentioned that we went water-skiing."

"Anything else?"

"No."

"What did the two of you talk about?"

A soft frown creased her forehead. "What an odd question. I'm afraid I don't really remember. Nothing out of the ordinary. Why do you ask?"

"Idle curiosity."

"No," Melina said, shaking her head. "It's more than that. You may be curious, but there's nothing idle about it."

His eyes narrowed. "Don't assume that you know me after only two days, Melina. That would be a mistake."

"Does anyone really know you, Aristo?"

"Does anyone ever really know anyone else? Human beings are complicated creatures. We let others see only what we want them to see."

"No," Melina disagreed quietly. "Most people don't have the kind of talent or energy that kind of deception requires."

"Are you saying that the Melina Chase seated across from me at this moment is the real Melina? No holds barred? What one sees is what one gets?"

Melina smiled. "I'm not quite as transparent as that. For instance, I have a temper, but I don't happen to be angry at the moment. I also have a sense of humor, but I'm not feeling particularly funny tonight. People who know me well have met most, if not all, of the characteristics that go into making me the way I am."

"No secrets?"

"We all have secrets."

"And what are yours?"

Her eyes met his for a long moment. They glowed tawny in the candlelight. "If I told you that, they wouldn't be secrets anymore, would they?"

"Does anyone know your secrets, Melina?"

She lowered her gaze again, afraid he'd be able to read in her eyes what she was feeling. "No," she said softly.

Aristo finished his wine and put the glass on the table. "Come. I'll take you home."

As they rose to leave, the man who'd served them dinner walked onto the loggia. "You have a telephone call, Mr. Drapano."

Aristo excused himself and went into the villa. While the man cleared the table, Melina wandered over to the couch to wait, her head back against the cushion, her eyes on the moon, her mind deep in thought. She'd wanted to ask him about Lambus, but for some reason she hesitated. And she wanted to ask him why he'd spent the night watching the *Calista*, but didn't quite know how.

Her eyes slowly drifted closed. What with not having slept well and the wine with dinner, she didn't stand a chance.

Aristo returned to the loggia. "I'm sorry I took so long..." His eyes fell upon Melina, her legs curled up under her, her long hair over one shoulder. He hunkered down in front of her so that they were eye level and just looked at her.

If anyone who knew him had been there to see the depth of emotion in his eyes as he gazed at this woman, they would have been shocked.

"Melina?" he said softly.

She moved a little.

He traced her cheek with a gentle finger. "Melina?"

She slowly opened her sleepy eyes. It took her a moment to get her bearings. "Oh," she said as she started to sit up. "I'm sorry."

"That's all right."

"Are you ready to go?"

"We're not going anywhere. You're going to spend the night here."

"I can't, really. Luigi will be worried."

"Who's Luigi?"

"He works on the ship."

"I'll call him."

Melina stood up, still half asleep, and swayed. Aristo picked her up in his arms and carried her inside.

A WOMAN IN LOVE

He felt her body automatically stiffen. "Relax," he whispered against her hair. "I'm not going to bite you."

"I can walk."

"You can barely stand."

He was right. She gave up and leaned her head against his shoulder, sighing as she closed her eyes again. But sleepy or not, she was intensely aware of the solidity of his body wherever it touched hers, and of the heat that came from him and penetrated her clothes to bathe her own body.

He took her upstairs to a bedroom. Without turning on a light, he crossed the room, pulled back the bedcovers and placed her gently down.

Melina opened her eyes and watched him in the dim moonlight that filtered in through the unshuttered windows as he removed her shoes, then leaned over to cover her with the light blanket. He saw that her eyes were open and a slow smile curved his mouth. "It's just like old times, isn't it, Mary?"

Melina's lips softly parted. "You *did* remember!"

"Oh, yes. I remembered. This time, don't run away."

"I can't. You know where I live."

His eyes looked into hers. "I almost wish I'd known the last time. Maybe things would be different now."

He left the room and closed the door softly behind him. A moment later she heard the door to the next bedroom open and close. Melina turned her head and stared at the wall knowing that Aristo was beyond.

How symbolic, she thought.

Chapter Five

When Melina awoke, she had no idea what time it was. Only that it was still dark out. What had awakened her? A noise? Or had she dreamed it?

She lay still for a few minutes, listening. There was only silence. She tried closing her eyes and falling back to sleep, but it was hopeless. More in annoyance than anything else, she climbed out of bed and walked to the window to look out. It was only then that she realized Aristo had put her in the same room as he'd done all those years ago. With a reminiscent smile, she opened the door leading to the balcony and went down the steps.

The night air was crisp and perfect. She could still see the moon and there was no hint of sunrise, so it was probably no more than two or three o'clock in the morning.

With her hands in her pockets, Melina made her way to the cliffs and looked out to sea. The *Calista*, her "parking" lights on, drifted peacefully in the bay.

Something in the sea caught her eye. Melina moved a little closer to the edge of the cliff, her eyes narrowed in concentration. Her heart leaped when she saw it again. A light. Under the water not far from the *Calista*.

It disappeared, then came back and stayed. She watched it moving around, swinging this way and that. So this was the mysterious light that the islanders were talking about.

Racing back to the villa, she went up the stairs two at a time to her balcony, through her room and to the door of the one she'd heard Aristo enter. Melina knocked softly at first, then more loudly when there was no answer.

Opening the door a crack, she peeked in. "Aristo?" she said quietly.

No answer.

"Aristo?" she said a little more firmly as she entered the dark room.

There was still no answer.

Moving her hand along the wall, she found what she was looking for and flipped on the switch. An overhead light clicked on, rudely flooding the room with light. No one was there. The bed not only was empty but hadn't even been slept in.

Melina stood there for a moment, not quite knowing what to do. Maybe she'd only dreamed he'd come into this room. But she couldn't very well go walking around the villa in the middle of the night knocking on people's doors looking for Aristo. She started to leave, but stopped with a sudden thought and went back in. Feeling intrusive but forcing herself to do it anyway, Melina went to the closet and opened the door. Men's clothes hung there. She touched the sleeve of one jacket she recognized. It was Aristo's. So where was he?

Moving to the door, she stood for a moment looking around the masculine room with its dark woods and blue drapes before flicking off the switch. Closing the door behind her, she went to her room and back outside to the cliff, where she sat cross-legged on the ground near the edge and just watched.

There was no more light. No matter how hard she strained her eyes, Melina couldn't spot it anywhere.

She heard someone moving behind her before she saw him, and turned her head.

"What are you doing up at this hour?" Aristo asked as he sat beside her.

"Looking for you. I saw a light in the sea."

Aristo looked at her skeptically.

"I did! It wasn't too far from the *Calista*."

He focused on the water and just watched.

"It's gone now," Melina said after a few minutes. "But it was there. I went to your room to get you, but you weren't there." She looked at his wet hair.

"I was swimming."

"You were out there in the water and you didn't see anything?"

"I was on the other side of the cliff."

"Oh." Melina's voice echoed her disappointment.

He stared out at the water a little longer. "Maybe you just imagined you saw a light."

She shook her head. "No. It was there."

"Are you sure it wasn't the reflection of the moon?"

"Only if the moon fell into the sea and began reflecting upward."

Aristo grew silent.

"You know, it looked to me like an underwater spotlight. The kind people use for underwater photography or night work. But what would somebody be doing out there at this hour? And so near the *Calista*?" She turned to Aristo. "Do you suppose someone is tampering with the dig?"

"I doubt it."

"Nothing else makes any sense."

Aristo sighed. "Are you always so curious?"

"About things like this? Of course. Aren't you?"

"I think," he said as he rose to his feet, taking Melina's hand in his and pulling her up with him, "that there are some things best left alone."

"How can you say that? I think the police should be called."

The grip he had on her hand tightened. "No. Not the police."

"But..."

"I said, not the police. It was probably just a curious islander."

"Or maybe someone trying to work the Kortinians up over that curse again."

"Certainly that's a possibility."

Melina moved away from him, her eyes on his. "You know exactly what's going on, don't you?"

He said nothing.

"You know why my father's work here has been plagued with accidents and you know why my scuba gear failed."

"What makes you say that?"

"I can't prove it, of course. It's just a feeling."

"And do you often get these 'feelings'?"

"Lately, yes."

"And if I tell you that you're wrong?"

"I won't believe you."

A corner of his mouth lifted. "That's honest."

She looked at him pleadingly. "Won't you just tell me what you know?"

"I don't know anything."

"Would you tell me if you did?"

"If I were certain of my facts." He put his hand at her waist and turned her away from the cliff. "Come on. Let's go back inside."

They walked along together until they reached the stairs that led to Melina's room. She went up a few steps, but turned suddenly and looked at Aristo. "Can you at least tell me if it has something to do with the curse?"

He relented a little. "My best guess is that it doesn't."

"That's a relief, at least."

Aristo reached out as though he were going to touch her, but his hand fell back to his side. "Try to get a little more sleep before the sun comes up."

She started back up the steps.

"And Melina?"

She turned her head.

"Don't tell anyone what you told me tonight about seeing the light."

"I have to tell my father. Particularly since it might concern his work."

"All right, if you must, but no one else."

"If that's what you want."

"It is."

For once in her life, Melina didn't ask why. "All right."

"Good night."

"Good night."

When she was in her dark room, she looked out the window. As soon as Aristo thought she was in bed, he quickly strode off away from the villa.

Melina just stood there, watching. She was tempted to follow him, but something told her not to. Not tonight.

With a tired sigh, she lay on top of the bedcovers and stared at the ceiling. She had definitely landed in the middle of something.

Melina never did fall asleep again, but lay still listening for a sound that would tell her Aristo had returned to his room. The sound never came.

As soon as dawn arrived, she rose from the bed and went downstairs. The butler was already up and greeted her with a smile. "Good morning, miss."

She returned his smile. "May I have some writing paper and a pen?" she asked.

"Of course. I'll just be a moment."

Melina went outside and sat on the loggia while she waited, listening to the birds as they came awake and went in search of breakfast.

The butler returned with some stationery and a pen and set them in front of her on the table. "Would you like anything else? Coffee? Something to eat?"

"No. This is all. Thank you."

With a slight inclination of his head, he went back inside while Melina picked up the pen and began a note to Aristo, thanking him for dinner and for letting her stay the night. Placing it in an envelope, she wrote his name on it and left it on the table.

Picking up the new air tank Aristo had left leaning against the wall last night, she shouldered it by the strap and left the villa to walk down the winding mountain road that led to the village. It took her about an hour to make the trip, but it was pleasant going. The sun was fully up by the time she arrived, and people were already busily setting up their stalls for business.

Walking directly to the waterfront, she found two young men—the same two who'd met Aristo's boat at the dock on the first day here—and asked them if they'd take her in their small boat out to the *Calista*. They agreed, and helped her into their boat. Within seconds they were on their way, their tiny outboard engine sounding like a bee as it skimmed over the sea.

They pulled up close to the ladder, and she had them wait while she ran down to her cabin for some money. As soon as she'd paid them, they headed back to Kortina.

Melina went back to her cabin, showered and changed into her bathing suit for another day of work. By the time she arrived on the upper deck the other divers were already there.

Craig spotted her and grinned. "Got back a little early this morning, didn't you?"

"It's not what you think."

His grin grew wider.

"And even if it were, it's none of your business."

"Consider me put in my place."

"I want you to have everyone check his equipment before he goes down."

"We always do."

"No, I don't mean superficially. They should really look closely."

His amusement faded. "What's going on?"

"I had some trouble with my tank and gauge yesterday."

He nodded. "All right. I'll take care of it."

"Is my dad here yet?"

"I haven't seen him if he is."

"He's not supposed to be. I was just hoping maybe he'd come back a little early."

"Are you diving with us today?"

"Uh-huh. The same area where my father put me before."

"Okay. I'll see you later." As he went off to get himself ready and to speak with the other divers, Melina climbed into her gear and went off the diving platform into the water.

She was the first one in, but rather than going straight to her grid she swam to where she thought she'd seen the light, about halfway between the *Calista* and shore.

Skimming over the floor of the sea, she looked closely, though for what she didn't know. The thing uppermost in her mind was that someone knew something about the underwater city. She knew, thanks largely to what Plato had written about a Kortina he'd never seen—a Kortina that had disappeared long before Plato was born—that great riches were believed to have been buried with the city. There had never been anything found over the centuries to substantiate this. It could well be that the ruins had been looted before Plato had even written about the disaster.

Nothing appeared to be disturbed, but someone very definitely had been there during the night. She'd seen the light. It hadn't been a dream. It had been there.

With a last look around, she made her way to her grid, picked up the suction lift and set to work. Pericles was already removing heavy stones. She didn't see the way he watched her.

It was a long day, but a productive one because she was able to clear another layer of sand away. She found some scattered pieces of pottery, which she placed in a basket nearby. If the weather held up and the sea stayed calm, she could make some real progress before leaving to go back to Cyprus.

It was early evening when Melina propelled herself to the surface and pulled herself onto the diving platform for the final time that day. A seaplane bobbed gently next to the platform, secured by ropes. Taking off her tank and other equipment, she left her things on the platform and climbed up to the ship. Her father was standing there speaking with an elegantly dressed man.

"Melina," he said with a smile, holding out his hand for her to join him. "I'd like you to meet Mr. Stratos Demopoulous. Stratos, this is my daughter, Melina."

The man was about Aristo's age, as Greek-looking as his name, with his dark hair brushed straight away from his olive complected face. He held out his hand and took hers in a firm grip, his eyes fastened on her face.

"Sorry about the water," she said as he released her damp hand.

"It's quite all right. I understand that you've been doing some diving for your father."

"A little."

"Stratos is considering investing in the project," her father told her, the excitement in his voice barely concealed.

"Ah," Melina said. "You're the reason Dad was in Athens."

"Yes." The Greek still hadn't taken his eyes from her.

She smiled, a little embarrassed by his blatant scrutiny. "If you'll excuse me, I'm going to dry off and put some clothes on."

"Will we be seeing you later?" Stratos asked.

"I'll be on the ship, if that's what you mean."

He inclined his head. As she walked away, Melina could still feel those eyes on her back.

As soon as she'd showered and dressed, she opened her cabin door and gasped as she nearly walked right into Craig.

"Whoa," he said with a laugh as he caught her by the shoulders. "I was just coming to get you."

"What for?"

"Your father wants to see you in his office."

"Is that Stratos Demopoulous still with him?"

"He's off on a tour of the ship. I guess he wants to see where all of his lovely money is going to be spent."

"If he decides to contribute."

"I think that's what your father wants to talk to you about."

"Why? What does it have to do with me?"

Craig shrugged. "Don't know. You'll have to tell me after you've spoken with him. See you later."

Craig went in one direction and Melina in the other as she climbed to the upper deck and went to her father's office near the front of the ship. He looked up from his desk and smiled as she walked in. "Craig said you wanted to see me."

Gregory Chase waved his daughter into a chair across from him, then rose and walked around the desk, half leaning against it and half sitting. "There's something I need to talk to you about."

"I'm listening."

"This is a little difficult."

Melina looked at him curiously and waited.

"Stratos wants to take you to dinner in Athens tonight. If you want to go, that's fine, but if not, I don't want you to feel in any way obligated."

"Has he threatened not to give you any money if I don't go?"

"No. But that wouldn't make any difference. I'd still tell you not to go if you didn't want to. I may need money, but not badly enough to exchange my daughter for it."

Melina stood up and kissed his cheek. "I know you'd never do anything like that. I'll wait until he asks me to decide."

"I meant what I said, Melina. Feel free to say no."

Stratos walked in at that moment. "I like your operation," he said to her father. "You're modern and organized, and if there's anything to be found, I believe you'll be the one to do it."

"Thank you."

"Less than a week from now I'm giving a special party in Athens. I'd like you and your entire crew to come."

"That's very generous of you," Dr. Chase said.

"Not at all. I happen to think projects like this deserve a wide base of support, not just one or two patrons. I know my other guests would be interested in meeting and speaking with all of you. Wonderful things could come out of something like that."

"Thank you. I'll see that everyone is there."

Stratos turned to Melina. "I was wondering, Miss Chase, if you'd do me the honor of having dinner with me this evening?"

Melina studied him for a moment. She didn't like the way he stared at her, but other than that, he seemed a perfectly pleasant man—interesting even. And just maybe, by having dinner with him, she could put on that little added pressure that would make him decide to be one of their more generous patrons. Her father might say he didn't need the help that badly, but she knew otherwise. Most of his own money had gone into fixing up the ship with the best of everything. Without proper funding, there was no way to pay the crew or buy the food. And maybe—just maybe—she could forget about Aristo for a little while.

"I'd like to have dinner with you, Mr. Demopoulous."

"Wonderful. And please, call me Stratos."

"Very well. And you must call me Melina. How should I dress?"

"The restaurant I intend taking you to is one of the finest in all of Greece."

Melina wasn't at all sure her wardrobe was up to it, but surely she could arrange something.

Stratos glanced at his watch. "We should leave here in about an hour."

"I'll be ready," she said as she went past him to the door.

He moved quickly around Melina and opened it for her. She smiled her thanks and went back to her cabin to canvas her wardrobe. She'd brought so little with her.

She pulled out the dress she'd worn to the Drapano party and rejected it. Then she dug into the closet of clothes she left here on a permanent basis and found something that was several years old but still, remarkably, in style. The teal-colored silk was perfect with her lightly tanned skin and similarly tinted eyes. A short-waisted jacket of matching color covered the spaghetti-strap top, and the skirt flared out slightly above her knee.

She didn't quite know what to do with her hair, so Melina brushed it straight back from her face and gathered it into an elegant twist at the base of her neck. As always, she used makeup sparingly, highlighting her eyes and cheekbones but in such a way that one noticed her features and not the fact that she was wearing makeup.

When she got to the upper deck, she found her father and date standing near the railing talking. Both men turned at her approach, but it was Stratos who stepped forward, his gaze missing nothing. He took her hands in both of his. "You look exquisite."

Melina smiled at him. "Thank you," she said as she looked over his shoulder at her father. "I'll see you later, Dad."

He returned her smile, but he didn't look too happy.

Stratos climbed onto the diving platform, then helped Melina down, holding her hand while she climbed into the plane. He climbed in after her and closed everything that needed to be closed while two of the divers who'd followed them onto the platform released the ropes. Within seconds they were moving over the water and finally lifting into the air, circling over the *Calista* and then flying over the island as they made their way toward Athens.

It was a shorter flight than Melina had expected—less than an hour. They landed on the water and taxied off the water and onto the tarmac at the airport. As they climbed out of the plane, a Mercedes pulled up next to them and a uniformed chauffeur stepped out to open the rear doors, first for Melina, then for Stratos.

As the two of them settled into the back seat, Stratos looked over at Melina. "Have you been to Athens before?"

"Many times. I think I've spent more time in Greece during my life than I have in America."

"Your father has a very great love for my country."

"I know. He always has."

"And that love has apparently rubbed off on you."

"Greece has a very rich history."

It grew dark as they sped along the highway toward Athens. Traffic grew progressively worse the closer they drew. Melina caught a glimpse of the Acropolis, beautifully lit to show the Parthenon and Erechtheum. Its beauty, as it always had and probably always would, brought her close to tears. Some people when they looked at it saw a ruin. Melina saw graceful columns and elegant architectural lines that had survived the centuries with dignity intact.

Stratos noticed her reaction. "You like our Acropolis, eh?"

"It takes my breath away," she said softly.

He gazed at her perfect profile and felt an emotion similar to Melina's.

The driver parked the big car in front of a flashy looking restaurant with a canopy that stretched from the building entrance all the way across the boulevardlike sidewalk to the street.

The driver opened the door for Stratos, then Stratos walked around the car and opened Melina's door, holding out his hand and helping her alight.

With his arm holding hers in a strangely possessive manner, he walked her into the restaurant. The captain knew Stratos well, addressing him respectfully by name before showing them to a table in a dimly lit corner.

Stratos seated Melina, then took the chair directly across from her. She gazed around the restaurant, vaguely disappointed. They might as well have been eating in Manhattan. Everything that could be done to eliminate the charm of the common Greek taverna had been done.

As her gaze came back to her companion, she was startled to find him watching her intently. "That's very disconcerting," she said with a smile to ease the coolness of her words.

"What is?"

"The way you look at me."

"A woman such as you must be used to men looking."

"You do it with a bit more boldness than I'm accustomed to."

"I'm honest. I find you to be one of the most beautiful women I've ever seen."

Melina had been told she was beautiful by other men and felt no embarrassment at his words. She met his gaze with a direct one of her own.

"What would you say if I asked you to be my mistress?"

Melina's mouth parted softly in amazement. "I'd say you were joking."

"And if I weren't joking?"

"Then I'd say no, thank you."

"Why?"

"Aside from the fact that I don't envision my future as being anyone's mistress, we barely know each other."

"So? I can offer you an unlimited future with wealth, position, power, whatever you want."

Melina shook her head, still not believing she was having this conversation. "Do you put all of your dates on the spot like this?"

Stratos smiled, flashing his white teeth. "As a matter of fact, I don't. But keep in mind that when I see something I want, I usually get it. And as it happens, Melina Chase, I want you."

"I'm a some*one*, not a some*thing*, and I'd like to change the subject."

He lifted his shoulders in a noncommittal shrug. "And so we shall—for now."

A wine steward came at that moment and served them a dry red wine that Stratos had apparently ordered in advance of their arrival. After testing it himself, Stratos gave his approval and the steward poured a glass for Melina and then Stratos. The Greek raised his glass to Melina. "To future liaisons."

Melina held her glass but didn't raise it.

Stratos looked at her, a smile behind his eyes. "I was referencing mine with your father."

"In that case," she said as she raised her glass to his, "to future liaisons."

Melina studied him over the rim of her glass as she sipped. She could see why women would find him attractive, though to be honest, she didn't particularly. He was also a bold man. She had to admit that she didn't dislike him for that. He spoke his mind, and he didn't seem to mind if she spoke hers.

As Melina set her glass down, she felt compelled to turn her head. When she did, she found herself looking directly into the angry tawny eyes of Aristo Drapano.

Chapter Six

The man with Aristo took his seat at the table, then Aristo walked over to Melina and Stratos. Melina smiled up at him, but her smile faded quickly.

Ignoring Stratos, who had risen at his approach, Aristo spoke directly to Melina. "What are you doing here?"

She was taken off guard by his anger. "Stratos—Mr. Demopoulous—invited me. Aristo Drapano, this is Stratos..."

"We know each other," he said tersely.

Melina looked at him curiously. Something was very, very wrong here.

"I'll speak with you later, Melina." Aristo turned to Stratos, stiffly inclined his dark head and went back to his own table.

Stratos resumed his seat, an amused smile playing at the corners of his mouth.

"What was that all about?" Melina asked.

"If I read Aristo Drapano correctly, he's not at all pleased that you're here with me."

"That doesn't make any sense."

"It does. You see, Aristo and I are what some might call business competitors. We both own banks here and abroad and have some other businesses in common."

Melina didn't say it, but she thought it would take a lot more than a little competition to cause Aristo to react like that. "How long have you two known each other?" she asked.

"Always. From the time we were kids. He's a little younger than I am, though not much. And he was always ambitious. He started out with just one bank that he took over when his father died, and built on that." He'd been watching Aristo as he spoke, but now he turned his attention back to Melina. "How do you happen to know him?"

"He was on the *Calista* the day I arrived."

"I see. Then he's a friend of your father's?"

"Not really a friend. More of an acquaintance."

"Is Aristo a friend of yours?"

"Yes."

"Have you met the rest of his family?"

"If by 'rest' you mean his grandmother and Timon, yes."

"What did you think of them?"

"I like them," she said abruptly. "Why are you asking me all these questions?"

Stratos shrugged. "Curiosity, I suppose. It's always wise to know as much as possible about one's enemies."

American music played softly in the background. Several couples moved onto the dance floor.

Stratos looked at her and held his hand across the table. "Dance with me, Melina."

Melina didn't want to dance with him, but short of saying she had a sprained ankle when he knew perfectly well she didn't, she had no choice. Walking around the other tables, they made their way to the dance floor. He pulled Melina into his arms, close but not too close, and they began moving in time to the music.

She studied his face while they were dancing. He was a very attractive man, but she wasn't at all drawn to him. If anything, she was slightly repelled, but at a loss to understand why.

Stratos saw her look and misread it completely as he smiled and pulled her closer. Her body automatically stiffened in resistance, and he responded to that by loosening his hold.

Over Stratos's shoulder, Melina could see Aristo watching the two of them, his tawny gaze enigmatic but intense. The man he was with had some papers spread on the table before him. He would speak and Aristo would answer, but his eyes remained on the dancing couple. She grew more and more uncomfortable. "Do you mind if we sit down?" she finally asked Stratos.

"You don't like dancing with me?"

"I think I'd just rather sit for now."

He inclined his head. "As you wish."

Melina did her best not to look at Aristo as they walked back to their table.

Almost as soon as they'd returned to their seats, a waiter approached to take their orders. Before Melina could say anything, Stratos had ordered for both of them. Melina started to protest, but closed her mouth over the words. She was here for her father. It was just one evening. For once she could let a man order for her without being difficult about it.

Stratos leaned back in his chair and studied the woman across from him. "Tell me about yourself, Melina. Are you involved with anyone at the current time?"

"Involved?"

"Romantically speaking."

"Ah. No."

"Wonderful."

Melina looked at him in undisguised surprise. "Wonderful?"

"Purely from a personal perspective," he explained with a wave of his hand. "That will make my quest that much easier."

"Your quest?" she asked.

"I already told you—I want you for my mistress."

Now she was beginning to mind his boldness. "And I already told you that I wasn't interested."

It was as though he didn't hear her. "Your father said that you were going to be here for three weeks."

"That's right."

"Three weeks is more than enough time for you to change your mind."

Melina smiled, trying to keep things light. "I think we've talked about this enough."

Stratos eyed her over the rim of his wine glass. "You don't fall in love easily, do you?"

"No."

"Have you ever been in love?"

She thought of Aristo, so close. "Once."

"When was that?"

"A long time ago. I was only fifteen."

"Anyone since then?"

"No."

"I find that intriguing."

"That wasn't my intention."

"I know. You were trying to let me down gently."

"Something like that."

"It didn't work. I'm a very determined man."

His words weren't particularly threatening, but his tone made her a little uncomfortable. "I assure you that I'm a woman of equal determination, and I'm not interested in developing a relationship with you."

Aristo approached the table at that moment. He stood looking down at her. "I'd like to dance with you, Melina."

She looked helplessly at him, wanting very much to dance but unwilling to be rude to her dinner partner.

Stratos came to her rescue. "Please," he said graciously, "I don't mind."

Melina thanked him with a smile as she placed her hand into Aristo's and walked with him to the dance floor.

Turning her into his arms, Aristo stood absolutely still for several seconds, glaring down at her, before finally moving in time to the slow music. "Why are you with him?" Anger was evident in his voice.

"You say that as though I shouldn't be."

"I think it's unwise."

"Why?"

"Because he's not the kind of man you should associate with."

"He's been very nice to me."

"Melina, Stratos is only nice to people when he wants something from them. Please, trust me on this."

"I do trust you." The corners of her mouth lifted. "I don't know why, but I always have. In this instance, though, you've misread the situation. I'm here with Stratos because I want something from him."

"What?"

"He's thinking of helping my father with funding and I thought my having dinner with him might help."

"Who invited whom?"

"He invited me."

He held her right hand closer to his body. "Melina, Stratos is a thief and a liar. I know he's also, at least according to some women, very charming. Don't allow yourself to be misled by him."

Her smile still hovered. "I'm not as naive as you seem to think, Aristo. And I have to admit that while I do find him somewhat charming, there's something about him that I don't like at all."

Now it was Aristo's turn to smile.

"May I ask what the problem between the two of you is?" Melina asked.

His smile faded. "Let's just say that Stratos and I don't see eye-to-eye on most things."

"He says it has to do with your competitive spirit."

"Does he?"

"Can you be more specific?"

"No, Melina. I don't want you caught in the middle."

"The middle of what?"

Aristo's gaze wandered over her face. "Oh, Melina," he said softly, "what a time you picked to come back into my life."

Just as he said the words and before she could respond, the music ended.

"I'll take you back to Stratos."

"But..."

Taking her hand in his, Aristo walked Melina back to the table. Again, with an inclination of his head toward Stratos, Aristo turned and left them.

Stratos watched her with interest. "Considering that you two just met, you seem to know each other quite well."

Melina didn't look at him. "I've spent some time at his villa visiting his grandmother," she explained as she spread her napkin on her lap.

"I see... Melina?"

She looked up at Stratos.

"You were off in another world."

"I'm sorry."

"It's quite all right. I do it myself at times."

Even as he spoke, their meals arrived. Just as there was nothing Greek about the restaurant, there was nothing Greek about the food. Her filet with béarnaise was done to perfection, as were the still crisp, unshelled sweet peas and cheese soufflé. Melina was hungry, as she always was after a day of diving, and ate every delicious bite.

"I like a woman to have a good appetite," Stratos told her approvingly. "Most American women of my acquaintance only pick at their food."

Melina sipped her wine, only half paying attention to his small talk. More to avoid having to talk herself than from a real interest in the subject, she said, "You've asked me about my life. Tell me about yours."

"I'm afraid it's a very dull story."

"Don't be modest. With all you've achieved that can hardly be the case. For instance, how did you acquire your first bank?"

"I had a little money that I managed to invest wisely. The owners of a certain bank in Athens, friends of mine, were having a problem and I made them a loan. When they couldn't repay it, I took over the bank."

Melina looked at him, genuinely shocked. "You did that to friends?"

His eyes were filled with mild amusement. "Don't look so surprised, Melina. They knew exactly what they were getting into. They needed financial backing and I gave it to them. They would have lost the bank if I hadn't."

"They lost it anyway."

"Because they had a debt they couldn't repay. It was their choice either to accept or decline my offer. Friendship or not, the financial dealings between us were strictly business."

Melina said nothing.

Stratos gazed at her, still with a half smile. "Do you disapprove?"

"It's not for me either to approve or disapprove."

"Perhaps not, but I'm curious."

Melina met his gaze with a direct one of her own. "All right. I think that if you'd really wanted to, you could have found another way. Perhaps offered them an extension."

"I could have."

"But you didn't because you knew before you ever made the loan that they wouldn't be able to repay it and you wanted that bank."

He lifted his wineglass in a half salute. "Very good. I did indeed."

"That's very cold-blooded."

"I repeat: That's business."

"Has your conscience ever bothered you over the years?"

"No. I haven't even had a twinge."

Melina shook her head.

"You're very softhearted, aren't you?"

"I don't know if it's softheartedness or if I simply have a different set of values from yours."

"Whatever it is, I approve." His gaze grew more intense. "You and I could have magnificent children together."

The surprise she felt at his remark was evident in her eyes. "I beg your pardon?"

"With my ambition, your sensitivity and our combined looks, our children would know no boundaries."

Melina smiled suddenly. "You should smile when you joke. For a minute I thought you were serious."

"What makes you believe I'm not?"

Her smile faded. "Because you don't know me at all."

"I know that I've wanted to possess you from the moment I saw you on your father's ship." There was no amusement in either his expression or his voice.

Melina literally felt the hair on the back of her neck rise. She snatched her hand from him.

Stratos watched her with a satisfied smile curving his mouth. "Would you care for some dessert, Melina?"

"No. I'd just like to go home."

"I know a nice little disco not far from here..."

"No. Please, just take me back to the *Calista*."

"As you wish." He signaled for the check. When it was paid, he pulled out her chair for her and put his hand on her elbow as he escorted her through the restaurant. When they passed Aristo's table, Melina's eyes met Aristo's. She masked her discomfort so that he wouldn't feel a need to come to her rescue.

And then they were past, but she still felt Aristo's gaze on her back.

Melina was silent on the flight home, intensely aware of Stratos's sidelong glances at her.

When the plane finally pulled alongside the *Calista*, Melina turned to him and extended her hand. She couldn't get away from him fast enough. "Thank you for the dinner, Stratos."

He took her hand in his and held it for a long moment. "I enjoyed being with you, Melina. Think about what I said."

"There's nothing to think about."

"One night with me and you'd never want Aristo Drapano again."

Her lips parted softly. "Aristo? What does he have to do with this?"

"Do you think I didn't notice how the two of you looked at each other?"

"We didn't look at each other in any particular way—not that it would be any of your business even if we had."

"He's nothing."

Melina retrieved her hand. "Good night."

Stratos's hand caught her arm as she was about to step from the plane. "He'll never have you."

"Let me go."

He held her a moment longer, then released his grip. She immediately stepped onto the diving platform.

Stratos leaned over the passenger seat and looked up at her. "I'll be seeing you again soon."

"No, you won't." There was no equivocation in her voice. She had no intention of ever setting eyes on him again. After slamming the door closed, she climbed up the ladder to the deck of the *Calista*.

As she stood watching him taxi away from the ship, her heart was pounding against her breast. Why had she ever agreed to go out with him? He was evil. There was no other way to describe what she felt about him. Not just because of what he did and what he said, but because of what she'd seen in his eyes. Melina couldn't remember ever having been that frightened of another person.

Stratos circled the plane in the water and sped past the ship as he lifted into the air. Only then did she relax a little. He was gone. She was home and she was safely away from him.

Relieved, Melina walked along the deck. She spotted her father's office light on and tapped on his door. He looked up from his desk with a smile and waved her in. "How did it go?" he asked as he leaned back in his chair.

She perched on the edge of the desk facing him. "I don't think you should accept his money."

"What?" he asked in surprise.

"I don't trust him."

Gregory Chase's eyes narrowed. "What did he do to you?"

"Nothing. He didn't do anything. It was what he said that made me uncomfortable."

"Such as?"

Melina shook her head. "I don't want to repeat it. I just want to forget it."

"Did he threaten you?"

"I felt threatened, but if you analyze what was said it would probably seem fairly innocuous."

Dr. Chase knew his daughter well. She wasn't a nervous kind of person. If Stratos made her uncomfortable—made her feel threatened—there was a good reason for it. "Melina, at this point I don't have a choice. If I don't get some money and get it soon, I'm going to have to shut down."

"It's that serious?"

He nodded.

Melina sighed. "I guess I could simply not see him again."

"That might help."

She gave her father a hug. "I'm sorry, Dad. I know you need all the help you can get."

"That's true enough. Did I tell you that Aristo offered me funding when I first got here?"

"No."

"Unfortunately, I had to turn him down."

"Why?"

"He'd attached an impossible condition to the money and I was left with no alternative."

"What condition?"

"That I back away from the dig for at least a month and take the ship away."

"Move this ship? Why?"

"He said something about giving the islanders time to get used to the idea of digging into the graves of their ancestors."

"If they haven't adjusted over the years you've been trying to get permission, one month certainly isn't going to make a difference."

"I know. That's why I think he had other reasons for asking me to do it."

"I wonder what they were?"

Dr. Chase lifted his shoulders. "I don't know. I turned him down at the time because I couldn't see disbanding the crew and moving everything at that point, but if I can't get the funding from anywhere else, I won't have a choice."

"Perhaps you could speak with him again."

"Perhaps."

"I trust him a lot more than Stratos."

"So do I."

Melina rose and walked over to a window to look outside. A helicopter flew overhead and disappeared as it landed on the island. She knew it was Aristo. She was glad he hadn't stayed in Athens.

She sighed as she gazed at the sky. Stars dotted the clear, black night. "It's such a beautiful evening. Perfect for swimming."

"I went earlier. The water's nice and warm."

She turned suddenly. "I just remembered something I wanted to tell you. Last night I stayed on Kortina and when I looked toward the *Calista* in the early hours of the morning, I spotted the underwater light the islanders have spoken of."

Her father frowned suddenly. "You did? Are you sure?"

Melina nodded. "There was no mistaking it."

"What did it seem to be to you?"

"Certainly not supernatural. My guess would be a diving light such as we use for night dives or deep water dives."

"So," he said thoughtfully, "we have a midnight diver."

"Apparently."

"It's no doubt someone who's just curious about what we're doing."

"That's what Aristo said."

"Aristo? You were with him when you saw it?"

She couldn't help the smile that tugged at her mouth at his tone. "It was all perfectly legitimate."

"I see."

"So, what are you going to do about it?"

"Do about what? Aristo or our night diver?" Dr. Chase replied.

"The night diver, of course."

"There's nothing I can do, short of staking him—or her—out, and frankly I think it would just be a waste of time. As long as they don't harm any of the work we're doing down there. They haven't so far."

"I suppose."

Gregory Chase watched his daughter for a moment. "Melina, how determined are you to dive while you're here?"

She looked at him curiously. "I'm enjoying myself, if that's what you're talking about. What do you mean by determined?"

"We're bringing up a lot of pottery shards and don't have anyone to put them together and date them. Since that's your specialty, I was wondering if you'd be willing to do that while you're here."

"I have only two and a half weeks left. That's not much time."

"I know, but I haven't been able to get anyone out here for that job yet. The best ones either don't want to live on a ship indefinitely or, like you, have other jobs they need to finish first."

"I'll do what I can."

"Thank you, dear."

She kissed his cheek. "See you in the morning."

Melina walked back out on the deck. Leaning over the railing, she tried to spot any kind of light below. She didn't really expect to see it, though, and she didn't. Aside from the fact that it was too early in the evening, she couldn't imagine that they'd be so predictable as to come two nights in a row.

Still, it wouldn't hurt to keep an eye out. Her father didn't seem to think there was anything menacing about the light, but Melina held a different opinion.

She smiled and shook her head. Lately it seemed as though everything had a menacing quality to it. She'd better watch her imagination.

Her eyes wandered to the villa. It was well lighted. Aristo was probably inside by now. Was he thinking about her?

She thought of his words as they danced. *Why did you pick now to come back into my life?* What had he meant? She was almost afraid to interpret it.

How long she stood there, lost in her thoughts, Melina didn't know. A sharp noise echoing across the water brought her out of her reverie. Then another one. Was someone hunting? At this hour?

She stood absolutely still, listening.

All she heard was silence.

Chapter Seven

Melina sat at a long table on the deck of the *Calista* patiently matching shards of pottery and piecing together what she could. It was difficult. Even though they'd been buried under layers of mud and sand, their edges had worn away, making any kind of perfect matching impossible. Some matchings were made easier by the fact that all of the pieces were found in close proximity, and the numbered pieces fitted together almost like a puzzle.

The work was painstakingly meticulous and at the end of the day her back and neck ached from hours of sitting and studying.

Craig walked out of the communications room. "How's it going?"

Melina leaned back and stretched, then rubbed the back of her neck. "Slowly."

A WOMAN IN LOVE

He looked at the piece she was working on and shook his head. "I couldn't do this kind of work."

"Too exciting for you?" Melina asked with a grin.

"Something like that. Have you seen Lambus? He's got a call."

"I'm afraid not." She looked at her watch. "It's getting close to dinnertime. He might be in the kitchen."

"I'll look there."

Pericles walked by with an armful of air tanks belonging to the divers and followed Craig down the stairs. A few minutes later, Lambus lumbered past and entered the communications room. When he came out less than a minute later, he looked right at Melina, and then quickly away.

Melina watched quietly. "He's a strange fellow," she told her father.

"You think so?"

"Uh-huh."

"Why?"

"I don't know. I suppose it's because he seems so secretive."

"Secretive? I can't say that I'd noticed."

"I wonder what he does when he's away from the ship?"

"I have no idea. My primary interest is in what he does when he's on the ship, and according to Luigi, he's a very good worker."

"I suppose." She wiped her hands on a small towel lying on the table. "I'm going to wash for dinner. What about you?"

"I'm going to eat a little later, after I finish my paperwork." He was already absorbed in the papers he held as he walked to his office.

After tossing the towel back onto the table, Melina went downstairs. Turning the corner, she nearly ran into Lambus as he was coming out of the infirmary. He had a first aid kit in his hand. Her eyes went right to it.

"Luigi cut himself," Lambus explained.

"Is it bad?"

"No, no. It's just a small cut." He started to walk away from her.

Melina followed. "I'll help you."

Lambus turned and shook his head. "Please, no. It's not necessary, Miss Chase. I can take care of it myself. You get ready for dinner."

"You're sure?"

"Yes. Please."

This time when he left, Melina didn't follow him, but she watched him until he was out of sight. She was right; he was a strange man.

With a shrug, she went to her room, showered and changed into a full white cotton skirt and short-sleeved muslin blouse, then joined the divers for dinner. The talk at the table that night was light and fun and Melina thoroughly enjoyed herself.

When she took her plate into the kitchen, she found Luigi sitting there eating his own dinner, a book open in front of him. "How's your cut?" she asked.

"My what?"

"Cut."

"I don't have no cut."

"But—" Melina cut herself off. Obviously Lambus had lied. But why?

"What makes you think I have a cut?"

"Oh," she said with a smile, "I apparently misunderstood. Where's Lambus?"

"He just left for a minute. You need to talk to him?"

"No. I, uh, dinner was wonderful, as usual."

Luigi beamed.

"Good night."

"Good night, little one. See you in the morning for breakfast, eh?"

Melina went to the upper deck and found a quiet, dark corner to sit in. The sun had set, but there was a spectacular moon that illuminated the sea. Melina stared at it, letting its silvery light wrap itself around her.

Some of the divers came onto the deck and sat or stood talking for a time, but they'd had a strenuous day, with another one to look forward to tomorrow, and one by one, they all drifted off to their cabins.

Melina's thoughts kept wandering to Aristo. She was beginning to think that the best thing she could do was end her vacation early and go back to Cyprus.

There was a movement on the deck and Lambus came into view. Melina instinctively drew further into the shadows of the ship, pulling her legs up under herself and sitting absolutely still. He glanced furtively around a few times as he lowered a launch into the water, then disappeared over the side of the ship. She kept waiting for the sound of an engine, but there was none. Curious, Melina carefully made her way to the edge of the deck and looked out. Lambus was rowing the launch with the emergency oars that each was equipped with. It wasn't until he was a good distance away that he started the engine.

This was more than Melina could stand. She lowered another launch into the water and followed, starting her engine immediately and steering around to the other side of the island, following in Lambus's wake. She had him in her sights when he approached a beach and she cut her engines, knowing that he'd be doing the same momentarily. Hers had been off for less than thirty seconds when Lambus cut his and there was nothing left but the sound of water surrounded by silence as Lambus climbed out and pulled the launch onto the beach.

There were no people here, and no houses. The rocky terrain made it less friendly than the rest of the island. She was partially hidden behind a large rock that protruded from the water. Other than that, all she could do was hope that if he looked out to sea, he didn't look too closely.

As she watched, Lambus shouldered a bag and headed inland over the rocks. Melina picked up her oars, pushed away from the rock and paddled to shore, beaching her launch some distance from Lambus's and hiding it among some bushes.

Heading in the same direction as Lambus, she clambered over the rocks, suddenly thankful that she'd had the foresight to wear practical shoes. He was lost from her sight, but she kept going in the same general direction until she came to a dirt road. There, in the distance, was an ancient temple, dedicated to Apollo, its ruins elegant in the moonlight.

And there was Lambus, walking quickly toward it.

Melina stayed to the side, knowing that if she could see Lambus so easily, anyone watching would be able to see her as well. The temple was on a slight hilltop and Lambus climbed up and disappeared inside.

Melina approached cautiously and looked around. Some columns still stood wonderfully whole. Others had toppled to the ground and broken into marble wheels scattered across the rocky ground. The stairs ran the entire length of the temple. She stepped onto the first one and stood still. There was a hushed silence around her, almost as though the ancient ghosts of the Greeks and their gods were waiting, listening. Nothing indicated the presence of another human being.

She climbed more stairs, until they leveled out into a grass-covered landing that stretched for about ten feet, then became stairs again. As she climbed the last of the stairs, her foot hit some pebbles and sent them flying noisily to the ground. Melina stopped and held her breath. Nothing.

Moving between two huge columns, she stood on the floor of the temple and looked around. Part of the ceiling still stood and blocked some of the moonlight, making it difficult to see. But she didn't sense that anyone was there.

Where could Lambus have gone?

The stone floor, with grass growing up from the cracks between the rectangular blocks, stretched forever. She moved halfway across, then stopped and listened.

No noise except what should have been there.

Melina had never been to this temple, but she'd read about it during her studies. She moved further across the floor, knowing there was a door somewhere... there it was. A black hole in the pale stone. She moved toward it, stopping at the head of the narrow staircase that led beneath the temple, and listened.

Very quietly, or so she thought, Melina started down, stopping every few steps, alert for any noise that didn't belong. Water dripped in the distance. Other than that, all was silent. Even the insect noises one would expect to hear at night were missing.

Swallowing hard, Melina went the rest of the way down. It was pitch black. A damp, musty smell assaulted her nose causing it to wrinkle in reaction. A hand suddenly reached out and grabbed her from behind, covering her mouth so that the scream that tore into her throat had no escape.

"What are you doing here?" Aristo's deep voice echoed off the walls.

As he released his hold on her, Melina turned, unable to see him. "Aristo?"

"I asked what you're doing here, Melina."

"I was following Lambus." She strained her eyes to no avail. "What are you doing here?"

"That doesn't matter. Why were you following Lambus?"

"Because he was up to something and I wanted to know what."

A WOMAN IN LOVE

She heard him sigh.

"He came down here," she said.

"I know."

"What do you want me to do with her?" Lambus's voice asked.

Melina moved closer to Aristo, her eyes searching the darkness for the man behind the voice. "What does he mean, do with me?"

"You shouldn't be here."

"Neither should anyone else. What's going on?"

"Go back to the ship," Aristo told her.

"No."

"Melina..."

"No. I'm not leaving until you tell me what's going on. Why are you in this place?"

"It's not your concern, Melina. Lambus will take you home."

"I already told you, Aristo, I'm not going."

"You are one of the most stubborn—" He dragged his fingers through his hair. "Come on. Let's at least go up where there's fresh air."

Melina reluctantly went up the stairs with Aristo in front of her and Lambus behind. As soon as she saw Aristo in the moonlight, she knew something was very very wrong. He looked terrible.

"Lambus," he said, "go see if anyone followed Melina."

"What about your arm?" he asked in Greek.

"You can take care of it when you get back."

Lambus set down the sack he was carrying, silently inclined his head and made his way across the temple and out of sight.

Melina moved closer to Aristo and for the first time noticed that his right sleeve was torn and bloody near the shoulder. "What happened to your arm?"

"I had an accident. Nothing serious."

"Let me see." She moved closer, but Aristo stepped away.

"It's nothing. Just leave it alone."

Her outstretched hand fell to her side. He looked so tired. "Aristo, I have no right to intrude on your life. I certainly don't want to be a burden. But I'm not a child you can simply send away with a wave of your hand. I'm here with you and I want to help. Let me."

"It's a long story."

"I have all night."

His eyes looked into hers. "Oh, Melina, I didn't want you dragged into this." He stood in front of her and placed his finger under her chin, tilting her face toward his. "You can't possibly know how I felt the day I saw you on your father's ship. Thoughts of you have haunted me ever since I found you by the side of the road and brought you to my home all those years ago. And suddenly, there you were. And there was nothing I could do about it then, and there's nothing I can do about it now."

Melina's heart was in her eyes. "I know," she said softly. "Just let me stay with you tonight."

"I can't risk anything happening to you."

She reached up and touched his face as their eyes met and held. "It's not your risk. It's mine. Now, take off your shirt."

"Melina..."

"Take it off."

Aristo, remarkably, did as he was told, unbuttoning it down his chest. Melina helped ease him out of it, then turned him toward the moonlight so she could see what she was dealing with. A strip of cloth had been wrapped around his upper arm in a makeshift bandage. She carefully undid it, trying not to notice that his mouth was etched with pain. "My God," she said softly when she saw the wound. "This isn't a scrape. What happened?"

"I got shot last night."

"Shot! Why? By whom?"

Aristo sighed.

"All right. Tell me later. First we've got to fix this arm. You're going to have to sit down."

Aristo moved near a column and leaned his back against it. Melina picked up the sack Lambus had been carrying and opened it. "I assume he brought the first aid kit I caught him with earlier." But what she pulled out was a bottle of liquor.

"What's that?" Aristo asked.

Melina struggled to see the label. "Brandy."

"Perfect. Remind me to thank Lambus when he comes back," he said as he took the bottle from her with his good hand. Raising it to his mouth, he pulled the cork out with his teeth and drank deeply. Leaning his head back against the column, Aristo closed his eyes.

Melina found the first aid kit, opened it and put it on the floor next to her, looking back and forth from its contents to the wound. "You should see a doctor."

"No doctor. Not yet, anyway."

"You could get an infection."

"That's a chance I have to take." He looked at her from the corner of his eye. "Do you know what you're doing?"

"No."

"That's encouraging."

"Don't get insulting. I'm all you've got at the moment."

Aristo smiled as he took another drink. A man could do worse.

Melina took a small bottle of disinfectant alcohol from the first aid kit and unscrewed the cap. "This might sting a bit," she said as she poured it directly over the wound.

Aristo swore and sat up straight as he looked at her accusingly. "Sting a bit? Where do you think my pain threshold is? On the moon?"

"I warned you."

"Well, that makes everything all right."

"I'm going to put on a little more." She followed her words with action as she poured a little more over the wound, her throat tightening at the thought of what she was doing to him.

"Why don't you just kill me and get it over with?" he asked between clenched teeth.

"I don't have to. You're doing a perfectly fine job of that yourself. Now be quiet and let me finish."

He leaned back against the column, but this time he followed her movements with suspicious eyes.

Melina unwound a long strip of gauze from a roll and circled it around his upper arm over a thick cotton pad she'd placed directly over the wound. "Hold the end."

While Aristo placed his fingers over the edge of the gauze, Melina snipped off some surgical tape and secured it.

"There," she said as she leaned back and looked at her handiwork. "I'll look at it again tomorrow when I can see better."

"Something to look forward to." Aristo watched Melina's downcast face, illuminated by the moonlight, as she put things back into the first aid kit. "Thank you," he said quietly.

She raised her eyes to his. "You're welcome."

"Did Lambus, by any chance, bring food?"

Melina went through the sack again and pulled out a candy bar. "I suppose he didn't want to take anything from the galley for fear of arousing suspicion," she said as she handed it to him. "Was that you who called him this evening?"

"Yes."

"How did you manage it?"

"I went into a house about half a mile from here without the owners knowing it."

Melina put everything back into the sack but the brandy, then sat across from Aristo so she could see his face. "All right. Now I'd like to hear how you got shot."

He dragged his fingers through his hair. Melina's eyes moved to his muscular chest as his skin glinted in the moonlight. "It has to do with those stolen gold bricks."

"What about them?"

"I was transferring them from one bank to another. No one but myself knew what the arrangements were—so I thought."

"Who else found out?"

"Timon. And he told Stratos. Unlike me, Timon has always considered Stratos his friend."

Melina was incredulous. "So Timon conspired with Stratos to steal the gold?"

Aristo shook his head. "No, no. I don't believe that for a minute."

Melina was confused. "If Stratos stole the gold, and you know he did it, why are the police concentrating their investigation on you? Why don't they just arrest Stratos?"

"On what evidence? You can be sure that gold is nowhere near him."

"Then how do you know he did it?"

"I can't explain to you how I know. Only that I do."

She accepted his word. "How is Timon involved?"

"As far as I can figure out from what he's said, he had too much to drink and was trying to play the big shot with Stratos. He's always been like a child in that regard. It's as though he's yelling at the world, 'Hey, look at me. See how important I am.'"

"You said 'as far as' you 'could figure out.' Can't Timon tell you exactly what happened?"

"He doesn't remember. He spent most of that night in a stupor. Frankly, at first I thought Timon had stolen the gold himself."

"Logically speaking, that actually makes more sense, even though he's your brother. Stratos has money of his own. Why would he want to steal from you?"

"Stratos didn't steal the gold for its value. That's just a pleasant aside. He stole it in order to ruin me. To ruin my entire family."

"Ruin you? I know it was a lot of money, but assuming you were insured, how could a theft ruin you?"

"That gold belonged to the Greek government. The minute word of the theft got out, my credibility was ruined. I was immediately under suspicion of having stolen it myself. I still am."

"But why?"

"It gets back to my being the only one who knew the transporting arrangements, except for Timon. And I have no intention of telling the police that he knew."

"But his having told Stratos that information would serve to make Stratos a suspect."

Aristo shook his head. "It only makes us sound self-serving, not innocent. All Stratos has to do is say Timon is lying, that the conversation never took place. Timon can't even swear that it did because he can't really remember."

"Doesn't your reputation stand for anything? It's ridiculous to suspect you of stealing that gold."

Aristo smiled at her. "You have blind faith."

"In you I do."

"Thank you. But the sad fact is that not everyone feels that way. Oh, the people who know me well have stood by me, but that doesn't alter the fact that all of my banks have been steadily losing business to Stratos. And it doesn't alter the fact that there's a very real chance that either I, or Timon, or both of us, will end up in prison. It's all been finely choreographed."

Melina was quietly thoughtful. "I still don't understand why Stratos would want to do this to you."

"Revenge."

"For what?"

"It goes back a long way." His eyes met hers. "Stratos is my half-brother."

Melina's eyes widened. "What?"

"He, Timon and I share the same mother. She was married to his father first, then left him in order to marry my father when Stratos was only two. His father carried a deep hatred of my father with him to his grave and Stratos picked up where he left off. I sometimes think his entire reason for being is to take from me everything I care deeply about."

Melina was trying to absorb what she was hearing. "There has to be some way to prove that he took it."

"Only by catching him with it in his possession."

"But you don't even know where the gold is."

For the first time in the conversation, Aristo smiled. "Yes, I do. At least I think I do."

Melina's eyes suddenly lit up. "It's in the bay, isn't it?"

"I believe it is."

"Does Timon know?"

"Like me, he suspects so. He's done some diving in the area trying to find it."

Aristo moved and closed his eyes for a moment as a wave of pain shot through his shoulder.

Melina handed him the bottle of brandy. "Here, take another drink. It's the only painkiller we have."

He did, and sighed.

"All right. Now I want to know how you got shot."

Aristo's eyes met hers. "Are you sure you want to hear this?" he asked quietly.

Melina nodded. "I've heard this much. I might as well hear the rest."

"Carelessness," he said after a short pause. "When I came back from Athens last night, I went down to my boat with the intention of doing some diving. As I was about to step onto my boat, someone shot me from behind. I spun around and went over the side of the dock into the water. There was another shot. That one missed me and I swam like mad to safety under the dock where I could get my head above the water without being seen. The person who shot me stayed for a long time, watching the water. When he didn't see anything after half an hour, he left."

Melina was horrified. This was something completely out of the realm of her reality. "Did you see who it was?"

Aristo's eyes met and held hers. "He works on the *Calista*, Melina. His name is Pericles."

Melina was too shocked to say anything for a moment. "Pericles? Are you sure?"

"I got a very good look at him."

"Why would Pericles want to kill you?"

"He must work for Stratos. He's no doubt also the one behind the series of accidents your father's dig has suffered, including the damage to your air tanks."

Melina shook her head. "I'm lost. It makes sense, if Stratos hates you as much as you believe, that he would have Pericles shoot you. But why would Stratos have him get a job on the *Calista* in the first place? And why would he want to hurt the dig, much less damage my air tanks when he had to know—or at least suspect—what the consequences would be? What could my father have done to deserve Stratos's enmity?"

"Let's take it from the beginning. First of all, I believe the gold is indeed in the bay. But it's a big bay, and I think that after Stratos and/or his henchmen dropped it into the water, they forgot exactly where and have been searching for it ever since. That was easy enough before your father showed up with his divers. They hadn't counted on an audience. Nor had they counted on the possibility that someone else would find the gold."

"Why do you suppose Stratos dropped it in the bay at all? Why not store it in his home or on his ship?"

"He couldn't, just in case someone decided to believe Timon and call for a search. Besides, the bay suits his sense of irony. What could be better than to put the source of my downfall in my own back yard, as it were? Your father wasn't there at the time and Stratos knew nothing about his negotiations with the government to uncover the sunken island."

Things were becoming increasingly clear. "So when my father did begin his dig, Stratos put Pericles on the ship to keep his eye on things and to make sure that my father didn't stumble upon the stolen gold."

"And more importantly, to have someone on the site who could look for it on Stratos's behalf."

"So Pericles is the one behind the underwater light."

Aristo nodded.

"But why the rash of accidents?"

"I think because Stratos wanted the *Calista* out of the bay so he could bring the gold up without being seen."

"You wanted the *Calista* out of the way as well," she reminded him.

"I was afraid that someone was really going to get hurt. I had Lambus hire on so he could keep an eye on things for me. Perhaps prevent accidents before they happened."

"I was wondering about that," Melina said quietly. "There's still something I don't understand, though. Stratos could have had you shot anytime. Why now?"

"Because I'm on to him and he knows it. I believe Timon. And I've been watching the bay. Mark my words, Melina, Stratos is getting ready to bring the gold up and he doesn't want any witnesses."

"But the *Calista* is still there."

"I must admit, that has me puzzled."

"Perhaps you're wrong about the timing."

Aristo shook his head. "No. I know Stratos. I know how he thinks. He's ready."

Melina's eyes suddenly grew wide. "Timon! If Stratos is after you, surely he's after Timon as well."

"Timon left for Italy late last night. With any luck, everything here will be settled before he gets back."

"That's a relief." Melina leaned forward, her elbows on her knees. "What's your grandmother going to think when you don't come home?"

"I've been known to go off on business trips without telling anyone, including my office, and for now that's what everyone will assume."

"So to Stratos's way of thinking, you're dead, Timon's out of reach and he can safely bring up the gold."

"Exactly."

"When and if he does, what are you going to do?"

"I'm going to be watching, and I'll follow it straight to Stratos."

"Not with your arm the way it is."

"Unless you know some miracle cure, Melina, I don't have a choice."

"But you do. You have me and you have Lambus. We can do the legwork for you."

A corner of his mouth lifted as his eyes rested on her. "You would, too, wouldn't you?"

"I can be sneaky."

"Yes," he said dryly. "I saw how skilled at that you were tonight when you followed Lambus here."

Melina's cheeks colored in the darkness. "My foot hit some pebbles," she said defensively.

Aristo gazed tenderly into her eyes. "Melina, please understand. This isn't something I can let you do. It's not a game. It's life and death."

"I know that."

"Then understand also that I don't want anything to happen to you."

"Then you know how I feel," she said softly.

She could see the muscle in his cheek clench in the moonlight. "Oh, yes, I know."

"I wish you'd call the police in on this."

"I can't. Not until I can prove what I suspect."

"What about my father? Perhaps there's something he can do to help."

"Melina, what I've told you, I've told you in strictest confidence. No one else, including your father, is to find out about this. The fewer people who know about this, the less chance there is that Stratos will be warned."

"All right," Melina agreed reluctantly. "But I don't like it."

Lambus walked quietly across the temple to where they sat. "No one followed."

Aristo tore his eyes from Melina's. "Good. Go to a spot near the bay and keep watch for the night. Then at daybreak, come back here to get Melina."

Again, Lambus inclined his head and left.

Melina studied Aristo's face in the moonlight. "Thank you."

"I figured you wouldn't go back if I told you to."

"That's right." She reached out a gentle hand and touched his drawn face. "You look so tired."

"I am. Like I've never been before."

She moved over next to him and leaned her back against the column. "Put your head on my lap."

His tawny eyes looked into hers, then Aristo stretched his long body out on the hard floor and lay with the back of his head in her lap. He cradled one of her hands against his chest so that she could feel his heart beat. With the other hand she trailed her fingers through his thick hair.

He lay looking up at her.

"What are you thinking?" she said quietly.

"That it's going to be difficult to say 'goodbye' to you when the time comes. And it will come, Melina. You'll go back to your work, and I'll be marrying Helen."

Melina didn't speak for a moment. "I know."

"Don't lose track of that."

"I won't."

His eyes slowly began to close. "I'm sorry I got you involved in all of this."

Melina's eyes roamed over his face. Less than two weeks. That's all the time she was going to have with him. And even that would be sporadic.

Less than two weeks, and it would have to last her a lifetime.

Aristo's breathing grew deep and even. His heart beat steadily beneath her hand. What a work of art he was. Like a Greek statue come magnificently to life.

Leaning her head back against the column, Melina stared blankly into the distance. There had to be something she could do to help. Aristo was in no condition to go after a thief and would-be murderer, no matter what he thought.

Suddenly two cats screeched and hissed at each other. Melina jumped and looked in the direction of the noise. Nothing else moved. The cats grew silent.

Aristo turned his head toward her, but he was still asleep. She touched his hair again and relaxed. No one knew where they were except Lambus. They were both safe for now.

Chapter Eight

The sun was just starting to rise when Melina awoke. She opened her eyes slowly and tried to get her bearings.

Aristo's head moved in her lap. She looked down at him and smiled. Her hand was still in his, resting against his chest. But then her smile faded. She thought of a line of ancient Greek poetry that went something like "all the while, believe me, I prayed our night would last twice as long." This was her night with the man she loved. Her only night. When she left him today, it could well be the last time she'd ever see him. The thought filled her with indescribable pain.

"We have to go," Lambus said quietly.

Melina looked up at him, startled. "How long have you been here?"

"Just a few minutes. It's getting late."

"I know. Aristo," she said softly.

"Ummm."

"I have to go."

He opened his eyes and looked up at her. "What time is it?"

"I'd guess about four-thirty."

He sat up and winced as soon as he moved his arm.

Melina kneeled next to him. "I want to change the dressing before I go."

"You don't have time."

"Then I'll make the time. Sit still."

Aristo watched her bent head as she worked in the light of the barely visible sunrise.

"I'm afraid I'm going to have to douse you again," she warned as she removed the pad from over the wound.

"I'm ready for it this time."

Gritting her teeth, Melina poured the alcohol onto the wound. Aristo didn't flinch, but when she looked at him she could see the pain in his eyes. "I'm so sorry."

"It's all right."

"I wish you'd go to a doctor."

"I will, but not now."

Without saying anything else about it, Melina rebandaged his arm, then packed everything into Lambus's sack and set it against the column. "When I come back, I'll bring you some real food."

"I don't want you to come back."

"Aristo, I can't leave you like this."

"I'm fine."

"How fine can you be with a bullet wound in your arm and no food?"

"Melina—"

She lifted her hand and turned her head away as she rose to her feet. "All right."

Aristo rose also and looked at the other man without saying anything. Lambus turned and moved to the far side of the temple. "Melina," he said softly, "look at me."

Melina, her back to him, shook her head. She wasn't trying to be difficult. She simply didn't want him to see how close to tears she was.

Aristo's hands lightly touched her shoulders and turned her around. He placed his finger under her chin and raised her reluctant face to his. "I have loved you from the first moment I saw you." His eyes roamed over her face. "You were so young. I couldn't have you then and I can't have you now. I have an obligation to Helen and her family. She's a good woman, and I've made promises to her that I can't back out on. Not even for the love of you. I can't do that to her, and I can't do that to us."

Melina swallowed hard and nodded.

"I think when you came back this time that I should have tried harder to stay away from you, but I couldn't. I wanted to be with you too much."

Melina still didn't say anything.

He gently wiped away a tear as it started down her cheek. "I'll always love you, Melina. It would be impossible not to. But I can't see you again. I have to go on with my life as it's now mapped out, and you have to go on with yours."

"I know." Her voice was barely above a whisper.

Unable to help himself, Aristo pulled her into his arms and held her.

"We must go now," Lambus said from behind them.

Melina stepped away from Aristo and looked into his eyes one last time. "I hope everything works out well for you. Take care of yourself. Take care of your arm. Goodbye." As Melina turned to leave, she was rather proud of herself for not breaking down. But it was a painful kind of pride.

Aristo watched until they'd disappeared into the dawn.

It was still a little difficult to see as Melina followed Lambus over the rocks to where their boats were. He put his into the water, then lifted Melina into his arms and carried her to set her inside the craft. Getting her boat, he tethered it to his so that it would trail behind them before climbing in next to Melina and starting the engine. Without using running lights, they made their way around the island to the bay. Lambus suddenly cut the engine, picked up the oars and began rowing to the still silent *Calista*.

Lambus stopped next to the diving platform. "You get on the ship while I take care of the launches."

Melina nodded and stepped out. Her foot was on the bottom rung of the ladder leading to the deck when she stopped and turned back to him. "Please take good care of Aristo."

Lambus's expression softened. "He'll be fine, Melina. I'll see to it."

Without saying anything else, Melina climbed the ladder and went to her room. No one else was up yet. Lying on her bed, she closed her eyes for just a minute and fell sound asleep.

It was after eight when Melina finally woke. She tore off her clothes and ran into the shower, put on some jeans and a comfortable short-sleeved blouse, and went up on deck.

Her father, standing near the railing going over some papers, looked up and smiled at her. "Well, hello, sleepyhead."

She flashed him an apologetic smile. "I'm sorry, Dad."

"Don't be. This is supposed to be your vacation."

"I know, but I said I'd help."

"Believe me, Melina, you're helping more than you know. I was looking at some of the pottery you managed to piece together yesterday and it's nothing short of remarkable."

"I'd love to take the credit, but it's not so remarkable, really. The pieces from that particular area are falling into place like a puzzle. I'm rather amazed that the shards from the broken vases have managed to stay in the same general area. You'd think they'd be all over the sea by now."

"It's about time we had some luck on this dig. Speaking of which, we seem to have come into another nice bit of it. I know this won't do much for you, dear, but Stratos has invited you, me and the entire crew of the *Calista* to go into Athens tonight to meet with a group of people interested in what we're doing. It could mean major funding."

She looked at him curiously. "I remember the invitation, and I wonder why he wants the entire crew?"

"He thinks it'll give his guests a whole new perspective on the dig to talk not just to the pencil pusher but to the people who are doing the actual diving."

"I see." And she did. With sudden and remarkable clarity. What a perfect way to get everyone off the *Calista*. Tonight must indeed be the night. She had to get word to Aristo.

"Will you be coming with us?" her father asked.

Melina shook her head. "I don't think so. I'm not really a member of the crew."

"I disagree. I know it's temporary, but you're very much a member of the crew. I understand, however, if you don't want to go, and it's all right."

Melina gazed around the deserted deck. "Are the divers already working?"

"Have been for more than an hour."

"What about Pericles?"

Her father looked at her curiously. "He's with the rest of the divers, of course. Why?"

"I was just wondering," she said nonchalantly. "Before I start working this morning, would you mind if I looked at your sonar pictures?"

"Of course not," Dr. Chase said absently, already lost in his papers. "Who knows? Maybe you'll see something I've missed. I have some things to do out here, but you know where they are."

Melina nodded. "Thanks." She went into his office and straight to a drafting table on the side where the pictures were spread out. There was a lot of light coming in through the window, but she turned on the table lamp anyway for a little extra help. What would ten million dollars' worth of gold bricks look like on sonar? There were all kinds of darkly shaded areas where things were. Rocks? Pottery? Columns? Floors?

They were all no doubt there. But what about the gold? She looked until her eyes blurred, but nothing leaped out at her. Maybe Aristo was wrong and it wasn't there at all.

Melina reached across the table and snapped off the light, then went downstairs to the kitchen where Luigi was clearing away the breakfast mess and preparing for lunch. The cook smiled when she walked in. "Would you like something to eat?"

"No, thank you."

He shook his head. "Melina, you're going to fade away to nothing."

"Not in this lifetime," she said with a smile as she looked around the galley. "Actually," she continued when she didn't see who she was looking for, "I want to talk to Lambus."

Luigi frowned suddenly. It was the same frown he'd had the day she arrived. "You anda me both."

"What do you mean?" she asked, already knowing the answer.

"I mean that he justa took off. He wasn't here to help with breakfast and he'sa not here to help with lunch. You can't trust anybody these days. No work ethic."

Melina's heart sank. How was she supposed to get word to Aristo without Lambus to help her? "Thanks, Luigi. I'm sorry about your new assistant."

"Me, too. He was a good worker."

Melina went back up on deck. There was only one course of action open to her. If Lambus was not able to deliver a message, she'd have to take it herself. Her father was still leaning against the railing. "Dad, I need to go into Kortina for a short while. May I use one of the launches?"

"Of course."

"Thanks." She lowered into the water by pulley the same boat she'd used the night before, noticing that the one Lambus had used was also there. If he hadn't taken a launch, how had he gotten away from the ship?

Climbing in, she headed across the bay to Kortina. She couldn't go around the island the way she had the night before because it would have looked odd from the ship. As she docked the boat, the same two boys who had helped her on the first day helped her now, taking the ropes and securing them, and getting the yellow scooter out of the front of the launch and onto the dock. She gave them each some money before heading across the island along its winding roads to the temple ruins.

When she finally arrived, she parked and quickly ran up the steps. The floor of the temple was deserted, which she'd expected, and she ran across to the doorway leading below. "Aristo?" she called softly into the darkness.

There was no answer.

"Aristo, I know I wasn't supposed to come back, but I have something important to tell you."

Still there was no answer.

Steeling herself against the darkness, Melina started down the stairs. Some light from the outside penetrated the stairwell and fanned out slightly at the bottom, but it was still difficult to see. "Aristo," she called out as she stopped at the bottom step, "if you're here, please answer me."

There was only silence.

Melina went back into the sunlight, crossed the temple floor and sat on one of the steps between two columns. She had no idea where else to look. Lambus was no doubt with him already. Perhaps Lambus had already known about Stratos's trying to get everyone off the ship tonight and had passed that information along to Aristo. Regardless, there was nothing she could do about it.

Getting to her feet, she went down the rest of the steps, climbed onto the scooter, aimed it toward town and took off.

When she got back to the ship, Melina immediately sat down at her table where the broken artifacts were and went to work. She tried to concentrate on what she was doing, but it was an almost impossible task. Piecing the shards together took patience, and that was one thing she simply didn't have at the moment.

The day was interminable. Every time a diver came up, Melina looked to see if it was Pericles. Sometimes it was and he would occasionally smile at her. It was all Melina could do to force herself to return the smile, but smile back she did. There was no way she was going to tip him off to the fact that they were on to him.

When the workday had ended and everyone was on board getting ready to go to Athens, Melina went to her own cabin to shower and change. She put on a casual teal cotton sundress with a full skirt and some flat, matching shoes, picked up her book and headed for the upper deck. Her father was already there, dressed in one of his two good suits and looking handsome even though the suit was at least ten years old. A seaplane large enough and then some to carry the entire crew floated nearby, sent by Stratos. One by one the divers arrived on the upper deck until they were all congregated there. Even Luigi was going to Athens.

Almost all the divers, Melina mentally corrected herself. Pericles was missing. At first Melina assumed he was simply taking his time in changing. She kept looking expectantly toward the staircase, but he never came.

"Melina," her father finally said after he'd spoken to her and she hadn't heard him, "you seem distracted."

"Where's Pericles?"

He smiled. "You certainly have a profound interest in his whereabouts today. He left for Kortina right after the last dive. Something about his mother being ill."

"He left?" Her heart moved into the vicinity of her throat and stayed there.

"That's right. He'll probably be back sometime in the morning. As a matter of fact, I don't imagine any of the rest of us will get back much before that. Will you be all right here alone? I could leave someone behind if you like."

"I'll be fine." She smiled reassuringly.

Her father was still uncomfortable. She was acting strangely. "Are you sure you're all right?"

"Positive. Really."

Melina watched while the crew climbed on board the seaplane. It circled away from the ship, then sped past and lifted into the air. She raised her hand in a wave until they were in the air, then leaned on the railing with her elbows and looked across the bay to Kortina. It was a quiet evening. The water was almost glassy in its stillness. It made her feel a little better just to look at it.

Wandering around the deck, she stopped here and there, then finally picked up her book, curled up in a deck chair and began to read. Or at least tried to. Her eyes kept moving to the water beyond the deck, her ears alert for the least sound that didn't belong.

Melina's eyes grew heavy. She'd had very little sleep since arriving. As she allowed her lids to drift closed, she told herself that since she was on deck she'd immediately hear anything out of the ordinary.

What she didn't count on was how deeply she'd sleep. And how long.

It was twelve o'clock when Melina awoke. It took her a moment to get her bearings. When she moved, the book fell from her lap onto the deck with a thud that brought her fully awake.

She rose and started to go to the railing, but stopped and shrank back into the shadows. A fishing trawler was stopped about a hundred yards away, its wet nets glistening in the moonlight. It was an odd time for anyone to be fishing—at least if they were fishing for fish. Melina stayed where she was for a long time, her attention completely focused on the trawler.

Nets were constantly being lowered and raised. Very odd for fishing, considering that the trawler was dead in the water. That would seem to make net fishing difficult, if not impossible. She kept waiting for its engines to start and the trawler to move in order to drag the nets, but all was quiet. Still.

Something was very definitely not right. Melina began to watch more closely. She could see some activity on board the trawler, but not well enough to give her any clues as to what was going on. She moved closer to the railing to get a better look as some nets were raised and swung on board. Something inside the nets glinted in the moonlight, but that was all she could see before it was lowered to the deck. It could have been fish.

Or it could have been gold.

Melina's heart was suddenly pounding. Was Aristo watching? Did he know what was going on? What if he didn't? The answer to that was simple enough. Stratos would get away with it.

Melina had been raised to take control of situations, not let situations take control of her, and that's what she did now as she slipped out of her shoes, climbed down the diving platform and quietly lowered herself into the water. Her full skirt fanned out around her, floating on the surface until she began to move.

Swimming swiftly and silently, she approached the trawler, moving around to the side away from the *Calista*. Treading water, she waited and listened, then hauled herself out onto one of the large black tires roped to the trawler's side. Pulling herself to the top of the tire, she peered over the side onto the deck. There was only one man, in scuba gear, and he had his back to her. She couldn't see what he was doing.

When he finally moved, putting the steering room between them, she hauled herself onto the deck and stood there with water flooding from her dress and pooling at her feet. Moving swiftly to the wall of the steering room, she flattened herself against it, breathless and trying not to breathe all at the same time. It was hard to hear above the noise of her heart pounding in her ears.

The man came back. Melina turned and peered around the corner, watching. He used the winch to haul a second net on board. This time she could see. There were several moderately sized boxes made of metal. Whatever was in them was obviously very heavy. Another man joined him. It seemed to be all the two men could do to lift them out one at a time. Gold?

A diver climbed on board from the sea. As soon as he'd removed his mask, Melina recognized Pericles. "We have it all," he said in Greek to the other man. "Now let's get out of here."

When Melina would have jumped overboard, Pericles started walking around the trawler toward her. She ducked into the steering cabin, spotted a pile of blankets and dove under them.

She knew when Pericles had entered. She could feel his presence. The engines started without much trouble. The pistons knocked slowly, building up speed until the sound was fast and regular. Then the trawler moved.

Melina's heart was pounding like the pistons. What was she going to do now?

Aristo sat on the cliff watching the trawler through binoculars. His right arm hurt, but he forced himself to use it to hold the glasses to his eyes so that it wouldn't get stiff.

"This is it, Lambus," he said to the man next to him. "The only reason that trawler could possibly have for being in the bay at this hour is to get the gold. We were right all along."

Aristo spotted a movement alongside the boat and narrowed his eyes as he looked more closely. It looked like—no, it couldn't be. "Oh, my God," he whispered hoarsely. "What's she doing?"

Lambus, who was looking through his own binoculars, moved them around until he saw what Aristo was looking at.

Before their horrified eyes, a woman climbed out of the water and clung to a tire alongside the boat.

"Is that Melina?" Lambus asked.

"Who else would be crazy enough to do something like that?" Aristo shook his head. "I don't believe it."

As they watched, Melina climbed from the tire to the deck. He saw the diver climb on board. Then he saw first Melina disappear into the steering house and then a man. After that he had no idea what was happening. The engines started. He could hear them echoing across the bay. And Melina didn't come out.

He put the glasses down and got to his feet. "Lambus, you get the police in Athens. Take the helicopter. I'm going to try to get to my boat and follow the trawler. I'd almost bet that Stratos's ship is out there waiting for it."

"I should go with you. Even if you catch up to the trawler, what can you do with that arm?"

"I'll think of something. You just get the police. Follow in the same direction the trawler's traveling now."

Lambus nodded and left swiftly.

Aristo scrambled down to the rocky shoreline and made his way as quickly as he could to where he kept his boat, trying to keep one eye on his footing and the other on the trawler as it was disappearing into the distance.

The gold suddenly didn't seem so important anymore. But if anything happened to Melina...

He finally made it to his boat. The key, as always, was in the ignition. He turned it and nothing happened. Nothing. Not a sound. Swearing angrily, he grabbed a flashlight and set it on the seat while he pried away part of the dash. Setting that aside, he picked up the flashlight and focused it on the intricate arrangement of wires and fuses that filled the space.

Some wires hung down, loose, unattached to anything. The boat had obviously been tampered with.

He looked out to sea again. The trawler was just disappearing from sight. Trying to quell his panic, and silently cursing his brother for not leaving his boat docked where it should have been, Aristo got his tools and set to work.

Chapter Nine

Melina was still under the blankets when the engines stopped. She felt a bump when the tires along the trawler's side hit something, and several more bumps as the wave action of the sea pushed it again and again against whatever was out there.

She heard several pairs of feet hit the deck and men shouting back and forth. She not very daringly poked her nose out of the blanket in the darkened steering room. When she realized that she was completely alone, she exposed a little more of her face. Unless she missed her guess, they were docked beside Stratos's ship.

When it seemed that all of the activity was concentrated on the rear of the boat, Melina climbed out of the blankets and carefully, with just her forehead and eyes showing, looked out.

The activity was nothing short of frantic as men placed the crates full of their 'catch of the day' into the trawler's nets, raised them into the air and swung them over to the deck of the ship where another group of men unloaded them and sent the nets back for more. This went on for quite a while, and Melina crouched quietly and watched the entire time.

When the last load was swung onto the ship, some of the men climbed a ladder from the trawler to the ship, leaving only one man—at least only one that she could see—on the trawler. Another man with an envelope came from the ship to the trawler and handed it over to her lone companion before boarding the ship again. Melina guessed—correctly as it turned out—that the trawler would be pulling away. Just as the sailor came in one door—the one facing the ship—Melina slipped out through the other. There was no way she was going to let those crates out of her sight. No way.

The engine started, weak and knocking at first, and then gradually building up. Melina dove from the trawler, pushing herself out as far as she could before hitting the water in a racing dive. Moments later the trawler began to move. Melina took in some air and dove under the water, just in case someone was watching, and made her way to the side of the ship. After groping around for a moment, she found the ladder and climbed onto the bottom rung.

The way the ship was built, wide at the top, narrow at the bottom, she was able to cling to the ladder without anyone from the deck seeing her. She couldn't see them either, but she could hear them talking.

A wave slapped into her, nearly causing her to lose her balance, but she wrapped her arms around the ladder more securely and hung on. The hem of her dress floated on the surface.

She waited for the owners of the voices to leave, and after about ten minutes they did. She could hear their conversation fading away. Very cautiously, Melina climbed up the ladder. When she got to the top she peered over the side of the ship and instantly froze. A man walked past at that moment within five feet of her. If he had turned his head just a little to the right, with the moonlight the way it was, she would have been clearly visible to him, but his mind was obviously elsewhere, and his gaze remained straight ahead.

As soon as he'd passed—and her heart began beating again—Melina climbed on board and headed immediately for a wall. She knew there were a lot of people on the ship, but she didn't know how many and she didn't know where they were.

A cool ocean breeze whispered over Melina's wet skin and dress and sent a shiver through her body. She felt a sneeze coming and quickly pinched her nose until the sensation passed. What a time to catch a cold.

Just as she started to move, Melina heard someone whistling and quickly shrank back against the wall. A crew member walked jauntily past.

Putting her hand over her heart, she was absolutely still for a moment, and when she heard no further movement, she took off for the rear of the ship, still staying near the wall. She had to find a safe place to hide until she figured out what she was going to do.

The moon was just too bright for her to stay out in the open the way she was. Someone would be bound to see her sooner or later.

This time when she heard voices coming her way, there was a door to duck through. She closed it softly after herself and stood with her ear pressed against it, listening. They went on by.

Melina turned with a sigh, leaned her back against the door and looked at her new surroundings. She could see very little and she began to grope her way along the furniture to find her way. The side of her hand bumped against something and suddenly the motorized drapes that ran along three walls began to draw back. She hit the switch again and they stopped. Moonlight streamed in through the windows and she could see where she was. It was obviously a man's bedroom, enormous and dark. Stratos slept here, no doubt. When she pushed another switch the drapes slid closed. She leaned over to turn on a small bedside lamp, but before she could straighten, she felt someone touch her, just above the waist. Straightening slowly, she turned and found her eyes locked with those of one of the biggest dogs she'd ever seen. Her own eyes widened as she braced herself to run.

But the dog made no move toward her. He didn't growl. He just looked at her. Melina tentatively stretched out her hand and the dog rubbed his great head against it.

Smiling now, Melina sat on the edge of the bed—which put her almost eye level with the beast—and scratched him behind the ears. If there were a dog

A WOMAN IN LOVE

equivalent of purring, he would have been doing it. "Hello, fellow," she said softly. "Who are you?"

His nose nuzzled her hand.

With a sigh, Melina looked around. "I think I picked the wrong room to hide in. At some point Stratos will undoubtedly show up here, and I'd just as soon not be around when he does."

With a final scratch, Melina rose to go, turned out the light and went to the door. Looking out, she saw no one and cautiously made her way back along the ship, retracing steps she'd taken earlier. It was deserted. Almost as though the crew had done its work and was now in bed. Staying close to the wall, she moved quickly, stopping suddenly at the sound of footsteps behind her. There was nowhere to go. Melina froze.

A door next to her suddenly opened and a hand grabbed her, pulling her inside and covering her mouth before she could react. "Be quiet," a deliciously familiar voice whispered next to her ear.

The footsteps went on by and the hand on her mouth relaxed. The closet was pitch black, but Melina didn't need to see anything. She turned and threw her arms around Aristo's neck. His own arms closed around her. "What are you doing here?" she asked in a low voice.

"What am *I* doing here?" he asked incredulously.

"I suppose that could be thought an odd question, considering the circumstances," she allowed.

Aristo sighed. "Melina, you're something else. I nearly had a heart attack when I saw you climbing onto that trawler."

"You were watching?"

"Incredulously. What were you thinking of to pull a fool stunt like that?"

"I wanted to see what they were bringing onto the trawler."

"Did you?"

"Just the crates. Not what was in them."

"It had to be the gold."

"That's what I thought. I followed the crates here, but I don't know what they did with them."

"Melina, you should have stayed on the trawler and left when it did."

"And leave the crates behind?"

"Yes, leave the crates behind. That's exactly what you're going to do right now."

"And go where?"

"I left my boat anchored about five hundred yards from here. I want you to swim out to it and head back to Kortina."

"What about you?"

"I'm going to stay here and have it out with Stratos."

Melina moved away from him. "If you think I'm going to leave you here alone with a man who tried to have you killed, you've sadly misjudged me."

She could feel his smile through the darkness. "I don't think I've misjudged you at all. You're stubborn, interfering and you think you can make everything all right just by being around. It doesn't work that way, Melina. You have no business being here and you're going to leave, right now."

"And if I refuse?"

"Then I'll pick you up bodily and throw you over the side."

"You'd do that, too, wouldn't you?"

"I never make idle threats."

Melina sighed. "You leave me no choice."

"That was my intention."

He opened the door slightly and looked out. "It looks clear," he said as he took her hand. "Come on."

The sound of a helicopter had been coming closer and closer, and now, just as they were about to cross the deck to the railing, bright landing lights flashed onto the surface of the sea and headed for the ship.

Aristo swore under his breath and raced toward the front of the ship, towing Melina behind him. He took her into a large room and stood looking around in the dim light provided by the moon. She made out a semicircular bar with stools around it. Aristo had obviously been there before. He crossed the room to what looked to her like a mirrored wall, pressed a corner of it and it opened. He ushered Melina in, then followed her, closing the door all but a crack through which they could watch. Less than ten minutes later the lights went on in the salon and Stratos walked in with Pericles close behind.

"So our cargo has been loaded?" Stratos asked in Greek as he poured himself a drink.

"Yes, sir."

"Any problems?"

"No."

"Any sign of Melina Chase? She didn't show up at the dinner."

"No."

"Good."

Melina, her head just below Aristo's, watched as Stratos lowered himself into a chair and loosened his tie. "Now all we have to do is wait for our friends from Albania to show up, make the transfer and everything is back to normal."

"Except for your brother."

"Don't call him that."

There was a knock on the door. "Come in," Stratos said.

A man holding on a thick lead the huge dog Melina had met earlier walked in.

"Ah," Stratos said with a smile. "Come here, Caesar."

The man unfastened the lead and the dog trotted over to Stratos to sit obediently on the floor next to him.

The man left as Stratos sat absentmindedly stroking the dog. "The thing with Drapano was most unfortunate. I really would have preferred having him rot in prison."

"I told you that it was an accident," Pericles said.

"I know, I know. It just wasn't the way I had things planned. I only wanted him out of the way for a short while so we could bring up the cargo."

The dog grew restless and began roaming around the room. It seemed to sense Melina's presence and came to the door where she was. "Oh, no," Melina said under her breath. "Go away." She motioned at the dog with her hand. "Go on. Go away."

Caesar thought she was playing and began to get excited, whimpering and scratching at the door trying to open it wider.

"Caesar," Stratos called out. "Stop that."

But he didn't. Pericles watched the scene being played out and his expression grew suspicious. He moved toward the door. Melina could feel Aristo's body grow taut as it touched hers. He moved her behind him and waited. As soon as Pericles was close to the door, Aristo thrust it open, smashing it into the other man and sending him flying across the room into a table. Melina stayed where she was and watched as Stratos came at Aristo. She screamed and he turned in time.

Stratos got in a good blow and sent Aristo reeling. He hit his arm against the wall and a moment later Melina saw the blood coming through his shirtsleeve. Pericles came at him from behind. Melina moved into action. She picked up a vase from a table and raised it over her head, but caught a glimpse of it from the corner of her eye. It was ancient and priceless. She carefully put it down, picked up something else—an almost empty bottle Stratos had used to make his drink—and brought it down on the back of Pericles's head. He went down like a stone, leaving Aristo to grapple with Stratos.

For the first time, Melina saw that Stratos had a gun. Aristo's hand was around his wrist, holding Stratos's gun hand straight up in the air. The gun fired once and then a second time, then flew across the room and skittered across the floor.

Stratos hit Aristo's injured arm, sending him reeling backward. Melina then flew at Stratos, but he backhanded her and sent her slamming into a wall, dazing her.

Her next clear memory was of Aristo kneeling next to her. "Melina? Are you all right?"

She slowly focused on him. "I suppose so." Then she looked around. "What happened? Where's Stratos?"

Aristo inclined his head toward the floor where Stratos lay. "He should be out for a few minutes." Then he turned his attention back to Melina. "You took a pretty good fall. Are you sure you're all right?"

Melina smiled. "You worry too much."

Shaking his head, Aristo held out a hand to help her up. His other arm hung limply by his side. Melina went behind the bar and found a cotton towel. "Sit on the couch."

"What?"

"Sit on the couch. I have to stop the bleeding."

Aristo did as he was told. Melina sat next to him and wrapped the towel tightly around his arm. "There," she said when she was finished. "And this time you're going to a hospital."

The door crashed open and Lambus, followed by a herd of policemen, burst in. He looked around the wrecked room and shook his head. "I take it I'm a little late."

"Just a little." Aristo leaned weakly back against the couch. "The gold is on board somewhere."

The captain of the police moved in front of Lambus. "You don't know where?"

"That's right."

"And he stole it?" he asked as he pointed at Stratos.

"Right again."

Stratos moaned and came to. A policeman immediately moved forward and put handcuffs on him. As he was being led out, he stopped in front of Aristo. "You know, I was trying to get you in your Achilles' heel by taking away from you your money, your reputation and finally, your freedom. If only I'd known before all of this started that your real Achilles' heel is her." He turned his eyes on Melina. "Everything would have been so much simpler."

Melina automatically moved closer to Aristo. There was such menace emanating from Stratos.

The two of them watched until Stratos was out of sight, then Aristo looked at Melina. "He's right, you know," he said quietly.

Melina turned and met his gaze.

"I could have handled anything he threw at me, except if something had happened to you." He reached out with his good hand and caressed her face.

The police captain cleared his throat. "This is all very touching, I'm sure," he said in Greek, "but we have a lot of questions that need clearing up."

Aristo's eyes remained on Melina's face a moment longer, then he turned his attention to the policeman. "Of course."

"But first you have to get him to a hospital," Melina said. "He's had this wound for days and it needs to be taken care of."

"Yes, ma'am. We have a helicopter here."

As Aristo got to his feet, Melina came up with him. "I'd like to go, too, if I may," she requested.

"That's fine," the police captain said absently as he turned away to take care of Pericles.

"Melina," Aristo said as he looked down at her, "I don't think that's such a good idea."

"Why not?"

"Because I think parting will be easier for both of us if we just do it now. You should go back to the *Calista*."

"Parting from you isn't going to be easy under any circumstances," she said softly. "But if I have to, at least let me make sure that you're taken care of. I'll rest easier."

"You're a very difficult woman to say no to."

"Then say yes."

Against his better judgment, Aristo gazed into her eyes. "Yes."

Caesar bumped her hand with his nose. Melina looked down at him and stroked his head. "Captain, what are you going to do with Stratos's dog?"

"Have him put to sleep probably."

"Oh, no," she said softly as she hunkered down in front of the animal. "He didn't do anything wrong."

"It doesn't matter."

"Would you consider letting me have him?" she asked after a moment.

"You'll have to go through channels."

"Then that's what I'll do. Just make sure that nothing happens to him in the meantime."

"He'll be taken care of."

Melina looked up at Aristo and smiled.

The Greek's throat tightened as he watched her. How was he supposed to get through the rest of his life without her?

Chapter Ten

Melina had spent the night in the hospital with Aristo. He was still sleeping when she left to get some coffee. When she returned a few minutes later, it was to find Helen and her parents in his room.

Lambus, standing just outside, looked at her sympathetically. "I guess I should go," she said quietly.

He inclined his head. "I'll take you."

"That's not necessary."

"Yes, it is. Aristo put me on the *Calista* to watch after you and that's exactly what I intend to do."

With a faint smile, Melina set her coffee on a small table in the hallway. As she looked into the room one last time, Aristo looked up and directly into her eyes. Wordlessly, she turned to leave with Lambus.

It was afternoon when she finally arrived on the *Calista*. Her father came running out of his office and hauled her into his arms. "I didn't know what to think when you called last night. Are you all right?"

"I'm fine," she said quietly.

"What was that about Stratos and the gold?"

Melina stepped away from her father, her arms still on his shoulders. "It's a long story, Dad, and I'm just too tired to tell it right now. Would you mind if I went to my cabin for a while?"

"No, of course not. You can tell me later."

"Thank you."

"I would like an answer to my first question, though. Are you all right?"

She nodded and turned away.

When Melina got to her cabin she didn't even bother to take a shower; she was too tired. Still in her wrinkled dress, she lay on her bed and within seconds was sound asleep. Her exhausted body couldn't take any more.

She slept on, oblivious to the other sounds on the ship; oblivious to the hunger in her stomach; oblivious to the change from day to night to day. Her father came in several times to check on her, each time listening to her deep, even breathing, and quietly leaving again, closing the door softly behind him.

More than twenty-four hours passed before Melina was fully awake. She stripped off her dress and stepped into a shower, staying there until the cold spray stung her skin.

When she'd dried off, Melina put on a pair of jeans and an oversized sweater, packed her suitcase and went up on deck. She found her father sitting on a deck chair and sat down next to him.

He turned his head and looked at her with a smile. "Feeling better?"

"Much."

"Aristo called to see how you were doing. He told me what happened."

"I see. Did he say how he was?"

"No."

Melina turned her gaze to the sea, and beyond that to Kortina. "What about Timon? Did he get into trouble with the police for his involvement with Stratos?"

"Apparently nothing more than a slap on the wrist. I think his worst punishment is that he comes off looking like such a fool."

"He was one."

"Well, be that as it may, he's left Greece. I don't imagine he'll be coming back anytime soon."

"Speaking of leaving, I thought I'd go to Cyprus today."

Her father nodded. "I thought you might be."

"I'm beginning to think that vacations are more exhausting than work."

"Yours certainly has been." He watched her profile and his expression filled with pain. He was suffering the dilemma of parents the world over, wanting to help his child and yet unable to do so. "Lambus is on board."

"Why?"

"He seems determined to stay here as long as you're here."

"Maybe he wouldn't mind taking me to Cyprus, then."

Her father looked up. "Here he is. You can ask him yourself."

Before Melina could ask, Lambus answered. "Of course I'll take you. When would you like to leave?"

"As soon as I've checked on Caesar."

"I've already done that. The police won't release him yet."

"They aren't going to hurt him, are they?"

"No. Actually, there's nothing they can do with him at the moment except take care of him."

"Did they find the gold?" she asked.

"Hidden under a false floor."

"So Aristo's in the clear?"

"Completely."

"Good. I guess I can go, then. I'm already packed."

"Where's your luggage?" Lambus asked.

"In my cabin."

"I'll get it for you."

As soon as he'd gone, Melina turned to her father. "I'm sorry we didn't get to see more of each other."

"We'll make up for it on your next visit."

Melina nodded as she rose. Her father rose also and pulled her into his arms. "Don't eat your heart out over Aristo. He's a good man, but there are other good men in the world."

"I know."

Her father sighed as he held her away from him and looked into her eyes—so much like the eyes of her mother. "I'm sorry. That was a silly thing to say. I know that no one can ever replace Aristo for you, any more than I could love another woman as much as I loved your mother. I just hate to see you hurt."

"I'll get better," Melina told him reassuringly. "It's just too soon."

He nodded. "You take care of yourself."

"I will. You too."

Lambus appeared with her luggage. "Ready, Melina?"

She managed to smile at her father. "Write."

"I will."

Melina's gaze shifted to the Villa Drapano. She stood quietly for a moment and just looked at it, then slowly walked toward Lambus. "I'm ready."

Back on Cyprus, Melina's days fell into a predictable pattern. Her work at the small museum was absorbing, but then at the end of the day she had to go home and that's when she got trapped by her thoughts. Reading helped. Seeing friends helped. But nothing got rid of the persistent ache in her heart.

She'd been back for nearly a month when she left the museum one evening and began to walk to her small house. From seemingly out of nowhere, Caesar came barreling down the street toward her, nearly knocking her over in his enthusiasm. Melina, laughing, hunkered down and wrapped her arms around the dog's neck.

"I love a happy ending," came a voice from above her.

Melina grew still and raised her eyes to Aristo as he stood looking down at her. She slowly rose. "So do I. What are you doing here?"

"The police finally released Caesar into my custody. I thought I'd bring him to you."

Her hand rested on the dog's head. "Thank you."

Aristo's eyes roamed over her lovely face. "You look wonderful."

"So do you. How's your arm?"

"All better. The doctor said that if it hadn't been for what you did, I probably would have had a bad infection."

Melina nodded.

Aristo looked at her for a long moment. "I need to talk to you, Melina."

"No, I don't have time." The panic she felt was evident in her voice. "But I'd like to thank you for bringing Caesar. Goodbye."

She started to walk past him, but Aristo reached out and caught her arm. "I didn't marry Helen."

As Melina turned to look at him, surprise softly parted her lips. "What?"

"I couldn't."

"But you said..."

"I know what I said, and I know what I was thinking when I said it." An audience was beginning to collect around them. "Is there someplace where we can talk?" he asked.

"My house isn't far from here."

"Come on, then."

In silence, the two of them, with Caesar trotting happily beside them, went up the hill and down two streets before coming to Melina's small, whitewashed home. She unlocked the colorful wooden door and went in. Aristo and Caesar followed her. It was shadowed inside because she'd closed the shutters against the harsh afternoon sun, but she didn't notice that now as Aristo turned her to face him.

His eyes roamed over her face. "God, I've missed you." Melina started to speak, but Aristo touched his finger to her mouth. "After you returned here, I set up a meeting with Helen and her parents. I explained to all of them how I felt about you." His gaze grew more intense. "How I'd always felt about you. It cost me a small fortune to get out of the contract, but Helen preferred that over marrying a man who was in love with someone else. I'm free now."

Quick tears sprang to Melina's eyes.

A tender smile curved his mouth. "Don't cry."

"I can't help it."

Aristo pulled her into his arms and held her. It felt so right to hold her.

Melina's body melted against his. She raised her head from his shoulder and looked into his eyes. The love she saw there went straight to her heart.

Aristo's fingers tangled in her hair. "Marry me, Melina. Right now. Tonight. I don't want to be without you a minute longer."

When his mouth came down on hers, Melina and Aristo both erupted with the passion that had been building in them. They couldn't get close enough. His mouth left hers to explore the smooth line of her throat. Melina dropped her head back and a soft moan escaped her lips as his hands skillfully unbuttoned her blouse and his mouth followed not far behind. Her fingers locked behind his head, pressing his mouth against the soft swell of her breast.

Aristo straightened and captured her mouth again. He lifted her into his arms and started to carry her to the bedroom, but stopped suddenly and, still holding her, buried his face in her neck and shook his head.

"What's wrong?"

"This." He raised his head and looked into her eyes. "I love you more than I ever thought it possible to love anyone. And I want to make love to you so badly right now it hurts. But when we join together for the first time, I want us to be man and wife."

Melina touched his face with a gentle hand and smiled. "I wonder how it was that I had the good sense at fifteen to fall in love with you."

"Good sense and very nearly bad fortune. I came so close to losing you," Aristo said softly as he gazed into her eyes. "If you hadn't come to visit your father when you did, we wouldn't be together now."

"It must have been fate."

He shook his head as he looked at her in something akin to wonder. "You're such a miracle. Even when it looked as though we couldn't be together, you were there for me when I needed you."

"Even when you thought you didn't."

"Why?" he asked.

"Because I was a woman in love," she whispered against his mouth. "I still am."

* * * * *

Silhouette Special Edition presents

★ LOVE AND GLORY ★

from
Lindsay McKenna

Introducing a gripping new series celebrating our men—and women—in uniform. Meet the Trayherns, a military family as proud and colorful as the American flag, a family fighting the shadow of dishonor, a family determined to triumph—with
LOVE AND GLORY!

June: **A QUESTION OF HONOR** (SE #529) leads the fast-paced excitement. When Coast Guard officer Noah Trayhern offers Kit Anderson a safe house, he unwittingly endangers his own guarded emotions.

July: **NO SURRENDER** (SE #535) Navy pilot Alyssa Trayhern's assignment with arrogant jet jockey Clay Cantrell threatens her career—and her heart—with a crash landing!

August: **RETURN OF A HERO** (SE #541) Strike up the band to welcome home a man whose top-secret reappearance will make headline news... with a delicate, daring woman by his side.

If you missed any of the LOVE AND GLORY titles send your name, address and zip or postal code, along with a check or money order for $2.95 for each book ordered, plus 75¢ postage and handling, payable to Silhouette Reader Service to:

In Canada	In USA
P.O. Box 609	901 Furhmann Blvd.
Fort Erie, Ontario	P.O. Box 1396
L2A 5X3	Buffalo, NY 14269-1396

Please specify book title with your order.

LG-1A

Silhouette Intimate Moments

NOW APPEARING!
LIEUTENANT GABRIEL RODRIGUEZ
in
Something of Heaven

From his first appearance in Marilyn Pappano's popular *Guilt by Association*, Lieutenant Gabriel Rodriguez captured readers' hearts. Your letters poured in, asking to see this dynamic man reappear—this time as the hero of his own book. This month, all your wishes come true in *Something of Heaven* (IM #294), Marilyn Pappano's latest romantic tour de force.

Gabriel longs to win back the love of Rachel Martinez, who once filled his arms and brought beauty to his lonely nights. Then he drove her away, unable to face the power of his feelings and the cruelty of fate. That same fate has given him a second chance with Rachel, but to take advantage of it, he will have to trust her with his darkest secret: somewhere in the world, Gabriel may have a son. Long before he knew Rachel, there was another woman, a woman who repaid his love with lies—and ran away to bear their child alone. Rachel is the only one who can find that child for him, but if he asks her, will he lose her love forever or, together, will they find *Something of Heaven*?

This month only, read *Something of Heaven* and follow Gabriel on the road to happiness.

Silhouette Intimate Moments
Where the Romance Never Ends

IM294-1A

You'll flip... your pages won't!
Read paperbacks *hands-free* with

Book Mate · I

The perfect "mate" for all your romance paperbacks
Traveling • Vacationing • At Work • In Bed • Studying • Cooking • Eating

Perfect size for all standard paperbacks, this wonderful invention makes reading a pure pleasure! Ingenious design holds paperback books OPEN and FLAT so even wind can't ruffle pages — leaves your hands free to do other things. Reinforced, wipe-clean vinyl-covered holder flexes to let you turn pages without undoing the strap... supports paperbacks so well, they have the strength of hardcovers!

Pages turn WITHOUT opening the strap

SEE-THROUGH STRAP

Reinforced back stays flat

Built in bookmark

BOOK MARK

BACK COVER HOLDING STRIP

10 x 7¼ opened
Snaps closed for easy carrying, too

Available now. Send your name, address, and zip code, along with a check or money order for just $5.95 + .75¢ for postage & handling (for a total of $6.70) payable to Reader Service to:

Reader Service
Bookmate Offer
901 Fuhrmann Blvd.
P.O. Box 1396
Buffalo, N.Y. 14269-1396

Offer not available in Canada
*New York and Iowa residents add appropriate sales tax.

Silhouette Intimate Moments

NORA ROBERTS
brings you the first
Award of Excellence title
Gabriel's Angel
coming in August from
Silhouette Intimate Moments

They were on a collision course with love....

Laura Malone was alone, scared—and pregnant. She was running for the sake of her child. Gabriel Bradley had his own problems. He had neither the need nor the inclination to get involved in someone else's.

But Laura was like no other woman... and she needed him. Soon Gabe was willing to risk all for the heaven of her arms.

The Award of Excellence is given to one specially selected title per month. Look for the second Award of Excellence title, coming out in September from Silhouette Romance—**SUTTON'S WAY**
by Diana Palmer

Im 300-1

The heat wave coming your way has arrived...

SILHOUETTE SUMMER Sizzlers

Whether in the sun or on the run, take a mini-vacation with these three original stories in one compact volume written by three top romance authors—

Nora Roberts
Parris Afton Bonds
Kathleen Korbel

Indulge yourself in steamy romantic summertime reading—

Summer was never so sizzling!

Available NOW!

SIZ-1B